LOVE KNOCKOUT

LOVE, THE SERIES BOOK 2

AUBREÉ PYNN

B. LOVE PUBLICATIONS

ROUND FOR ROUND [WREN'S INTRO]

It's been a minute since I kicked it and just kept it real
It's not over but I choose how I choose to deal
I'll leave before there's cuts to heal
Before I have remnants of your love etched permanently on my skin
I'll end it now before I feel empty and used
Before you join the club of me too's
Long list of discarded healing tools
Fools!
For mis-loving me when they couldn't see the depths of my treasure
But you've started to embed yourself in me
Mazed out and I can't see the forest for the trees
Only time can tell
I haven't been coping well

Round for round I've been going with you
Extending these pieces of my blessing
As if I have something to prove

I've said once before I'm everybody's type
An exclusive list of very few will tell you to believe the hype
But I ain't for everybody
So letting you back in could scar me
I've got wounds that haven't healed
Feelings still to feel
I'm trying to keep it real

I won't lay aside another ounce of my pride
When I think about the tears spilled for you
Memories of sadness dissolving on pillows
And sheets brand new

I'll go round for round with you
In this love bout 'til we're tired
And facing knockout

Readjusting my crown because this ain't it
It's peaceful and graceful and kind and shit
But I've been taking gut punches called love
When all I'd ever ask for is a bedtime booty rub
maybe a cuddle or a kiss
I refuse to grant you the permission to make me feel
insufficient
I won't tell you how badly you got me fucked up

Love's a game, and it don't play fair
But it's a game for two
If you knew what I know
You'd hope your luck don't run up
I've given all I can
Done all I can do
If it's a love knockout, then it's all on you!

Jess Words

APRIL 2015

PROLOGUE

$\mathcal{W}$ ren Franklin

INTOXICATED WASN'T EVEN THE WORD TO DESCRIBE exactly how drunk the three were. Brielle, Nadia, and Wren had been bar-hopping since 8. Initially, they were supposed to get a drink to calm Brielle down and send her back home to her husband. But, after the second round of drinks, and being distracted by perfect strangers, the trio followed them to three more bars, only to land in a club. This was Wren's suggestion, but Brielle quickly took over the evening. After an argument with Julian, Brielle stormed out the house, ending up at Nadia and Wren's apartment. Agreeing to blow off some steam with her, they were going to need all three brains to remember what happened tonight.

Brielle's Hennessy was kicking in and drowning her brain of any and all logical decision-making. She was the life of the party and, for sure, going to feel the consequences of this wild night tomorrow. Nothing about Brielle's demeanor screamed of remorse or worry that Julian and Roman were on their way to shut this party down.

Wren was enjoying herself more than Brielle and was standing up and twerking along with the music the DJ played. The way Brielle's body was rolling, twisting and shaking was guaranteed to end up bad. Wren was normally collected but, after several glasses of pineapple juice and Hennessy, her judgment was just as impaired as Brielle's. Nadia... Well, Nadia was silently enjoying her intoxication, sitting with her legs crossed, as she people watched. After sending multiple men away from her, she was content with Brielle's display of foolery and counting the time down until Julian agreed with Roman by his side.. Anything was liable to happen tonight, and it was about to go down rather quickly.

Brielle and Julian were having yet another standoff. He warned her not to go out, but here she was, shaking her ass without a care in the world, causing Nadia to whistle and count down the minutes before Julian would shut the club down to retrieve his wife. It was funny to her, the idea of a snatch-up happening to Brielle that she wasn't involved in. Nadia and Wren learned, early on, not to intervene in saving Brielle from her own demise. She was presented with options and she always chose the latter. It was almost like she was addicted to her own punishment. Nadia and Wren decided, a long time ago, that she was rolling on her own.

Just like Nadia had suspected, a blanket of groans fell over the nightclub as the DJ's music stopped and feedback screeched through the speakers. "Brielle Nicole!"

"Oh, shit," Wren slurred, hearing Julian's voice stopping the party. Kwame wasn't in town so Wren wouldn't hear his mouth. But, since Julian was here, he would dictate the rest of the night. Nadia already had her Uber booked and was planning to take Wren with her. Looking like a deer in headlights, Brielle froze from the ass-shaking, as Julian stalked towards their section. Hiding behind Nadia, Brielle peeked over her shoulder. Without hesitation, Julian and Roman entered the VIP Section.

"Ro, take them home," Julian ordered, grabbing Brielle by the arm. Instantly hearing Julian's orders, a grimace crossed Nadia's face as she shifted her eyes over to Roman.

"I can take myself home. Come on, Wren," Nadia tugged at Wren's arm before Julian held his hand up.

"I don't trust either one of you. Nadia, go get in your Uber. Roman, take Wren home. If they're together, they'll end up at another bar. I'm not hearing shit Kwame has to say behind Wren," Julian ordered, making both Nadia and Wren's face turn up. Picking her small frame up off the couch, Julian threw Brielle over his shoulder and ignored Nadia and Wren's objection, stomping towards the exit.

"Uhh! I'm cool," Wren objected being placed in someone's custody. "I'll take an Uber with Nadia." Slurring and staggering to her feet, Roman scoffed, lowly, in amusement.

"Yeah, you won't even make it out here to the Uber. Come on, girl! I got other shit to do," he ordered.

Biting her lip and looking at the familiar face through her drunken bifocals, she couldn't even deny that his unshaven caramel face, low fade and brute demeanor turned her on. It could've been the alcohol or it could've been the fact that she hadn't had much of a sex life. Either way, how she felt, right now, she had nothing to lose.

"I'll be waiting on you at the house," Nadia grunted, not feeling Julian's orders by a long shot but she was entirely too intoxicated to fight him on it. After making sure Wren was safe inside of the car with Roman, Nadia got inside her Uber and left.

Without further ado, Wren found herself sitting in the front seat of his 2014 GMC Denali. Nothing much was said between the two, except where she lived, which she slurred, "1245 Garrett Lane... it's close to the hill." Nodding, he glanced over at her a couple of times. The pink, off-the-shoulder dress she chose for the night hugged every curve of her body. Roman was enjoying the view, as was she. She bit her lip and lowly admired his chiseled arms and stern demeanor. Approaching the stop light, her drunken alter ego needed to make her move before it was too late. Granted, what was a one-night stand? She worked entirely too much to ever cross paths with him again. Her work schedule barely allowed her to be around the girls let alone any of her brother's friends.

As she lightly touched his arm, he snickered lowly at her. She made her advances clear, as she trailed her fingers down his arm, to his chest then his belt buckle. Jumping slightly at her assertiveness, he was turned on. Honestly, weighing his options, this could've turned out bad for him. But he was clearly unfocused as blood rushed to his lower region. There was a silent agreement made amongst the two. It wasn't long before they found themselves parked on a side road, out of sight from the street.

Inching her dress up her thighs, she straddled him with a devilish smirk on her face. She didn't need any foreplay; the liquor took care of that. Gently lowering her body on his, she began to rotate her hips. Matching her motion, he gripped her hips. The windows fogged up and their moans were like music.

"Fuck," he moaned as she sped up her ride to reach her peak. He soon followed, they unraveled and came back to their senses. No further words or looks were exchanged. When he pulled in front of her home, she opened her door and lowered her feet to the ground. Before turning to walk up the stairs, she smiled at the forbidden fruit she bit into. "Thanks for the ride."

The next morning, Wren woke up with a killer headache. Groaning as she sat up and pushed her hair out her face, she looked around to get her bearings. She was in Nadia's room. Typically, when she got drunk, she always ended up in bed with Nadia. Instead of complaining, Nadia rolled over to the other side of the bed and let her sleep. She never grew irritated with Wren's drunken nights or tried to kick Wren out. It was their thing.

Soon after standing to her feet, Wren shuffled down the hall, following the smell of pancakes and bacon. Nadia was in the kitchen, cursing to herself after being popped a few times by the bacon grease.

"Damn it," Nadia groaned, sticking her finger in her mouth. "That shit hurt."

From the sound of her voice, Nadia was just as hungover as Wren. Entering the kitchen, Wren groaned and leaned on the counter. "Don't say it."

"Say what?" Nadia asked innocently, turning the stove down and looking over her shoulder at Wren, still in her dress from the night before. "All I was going to say was thank you for cuddling with me last night."

"Funny, I don't even remember how I got in the house." Wren groaned and held her head.

Nadia smirked slyly and turned around fully to face her. "What do you remember?"

"Julian shutting the club down..."

"Bitch, you lie!" Nadia burst out laughing while Wren held her head tighter. "You don't remember getting in the bed and saying 'shit, I left my panties in his car.'"

"I didn't!" Wren's eyes grew big.

"Oh, baby, you did. Don't play innocent with me. I know you remember getting a ride and a *ride*, which was so stupid but Julian ain't the brightest crayon..."

Nadia was interrupted by a knock at the front door, "I'll get it. There's Advil and coffee on the counter."

Nadia dragged herself to the front door and pulled it open. On the other said was Roman, with a nervous smile on his face. He held Advil in one hand and a Starbucks cup in the other. "Well, looky looky... A member of the creep squad has found himself on our doorstep."

"What's up, Nadia?" Roman looked over at her and shook his head. "Y'all were tore up last night."

"That wasn't the only thing that was torn up last night. She's in the kitchen."

Nadia stepped back and walked down the hall, leaving the two of them alone. Roman stepped into the house and closed the door behind him. He lightly stepped into the kitchen, feeling completely out of his element. This wasn't something he normally did. One-night stands were just that. He definitely took a page out of Kwame's book, with the way he handled women. But the way Wren handled him the night before had him ready to rethink his ways of dealing with women.

"Good morning," he spoke up, causing Wren to damn near jump out of her skin. Turning around slowly, she looked at him like she'd seen a ghost. "I don't usually do this but... I'm Roman...I mean you know that already. But I thought it was just proper to reintroduce myself. I'm sorry for rambling and being weird. I would like if you had dinner with me tomorrow..."

Although the two had met in passing before, this was the first time that Wren and Roman had been in the same space without Kwame. Roman was more nervous than he should've been, but he knew how Kwame was about Wren, which was why he stayed clear of her. Wren on the other hand, had a loss of words, realizing that she'd slept with her brother's best friend. Without so much as a second though the night before was putting her at a pause.

"Uhh..." Wren's sense was fleeting as she looked him over, without her drunken goggles on. He was captivating. The tattoos danced over the exposed parts of his body, his toffee-colored skin smelled like shea butter and his muscular build had Wren looking for another set of panties to hand over. "Uh huh."

She nodded her head, making Roman smile wide. "Here's something for your hangover and my number is on the side of the cup. I'll see you later." He bit down on his lip and smiled slightly.

"See you," was all Wren could get out her mouth before Roman saw himself out. Nadia waited until the door was closed to come back down the hall.

"Uh huh?" Nadia prompted. looking at Wren. She squinted her eyes and opened her mouth a little. "'See you...' That's all you could say to the man you rode like a bull without any inhibitions? Uh huh... I do hope you're more articulate before our date."

"I did not ride him like a bull," Wren defended.

Nadia smirked lightly and tilted her head to the side and glanced in amazement at Wren. "You forever amaze me. Might've not been a bull because you were torn up, but it was a ride... maybe like a horse?"

"Definitely rode a horse last night." Wren bit on her lip and grunted. "A stallion."

"Okay!" Nadia flailed her arms and grabbed a plate. "That is enough for me. Go and wash last night off of you. And while you're at it, you can wash my sheets, too."

"Don't act like you've never had anyone in that bed before me."

"I haven't. I leave them at their house to wake up and wonder where I ran off to and I never call again."

"You're worse than a man, I swear."

"Baby girl," Nadia smirked, fixing her food and shoving a piece of bacon in her mouth. "I am the man. No one will ever get a leg up on me. Follow me, kid, and you'll go places."

MARCH 2017

1

*R*oman Daniels

HE WATCHED WREN LIKE A HAWK, BUT HIS PRIDE WAS too high to step to her and end this silent war they were having, once and for all. She was surrounded by Brielle and Nadia. So it would be nearly impossible for him to approach her without commentary from the peanut gallery.

Everyone was gathered in Kwame's back yard for his housewarming party. He invited the entire crew and, surprisingly, Nadia had shown up. Of course, she came with a bottle for herself and not Kwame, but nonetheless, she was here. Roman drew his attention back from the group surrounding Wren, back to his target. He needed to figure out something to get her back on his side. It was going to take a great deal of planning and even better execution to make that happen.

"Stop looking. It's not going to happen," Julian chuckled, standing off to the side of him. "Kwame already told you to leave her alone, if you're not going to do or be anything significant."

"All of a sudden, it got really bright in here," Roman muttered to himself, shielding his eyes from Julian. "Damn, nigga! Do you turn down at all?"

"No, bitch. I'm godly," Julian smirked and lowered his body into the patio chair. "What's the game plan?"

"I don't have one yet."

Julian scoffed sharply at Roman's statement and picked up his beer off the table. "Would you use a coaster?!" Kwame shouted across the yard at Julian.

"You would think that he's the light skinned one," Roman chuckled and sat down next to Julian. "Kick your feet up. That's really going to send him over the top."

Julian smirked slyly and kicked his feet up on the table and watched as Kwame balled his mouth up. "He's about to end your life."

"I'm not scared of Nitro," Julian kissed his teeth and focused his attention back on Roman and his half-baked plan. "You need to come up with a fool-proof plan. Do you see who she's surrounded by? One of them is telling her to go find herself a newer nigga with more bread than you. And the other one is telling her to think about what she wants and weigh the options of being with you. Angel and the devil perched on each shoulder. So, what are you going to do?"

"I damn sure ain't about to get jacked up by Kwame." Roman sprang to his feet while Kwame barreled over to the two knuckle heads. Julian couldn't get up fast enough. Scrambling to stand to his feet, he ended up tripping over himself and losing his beer in the process. Everything started moving in slow motion as Kwame reached out and grabbed him by the collar and Roman watched the bottle of beer tumble and splash between the girls. The sound of shattering glass drew attention to Brielle, Nadia and Wren.

"My dreeeeess," Wren huffed, lifting up the hem of her dress. Stepping over the broken pieces of glass, she whipped her head around to see the three stooges looking at them with a dumbfounded expression.

"Y'all play entirely too damn much," Nadia groaned, stepping over the broken glass. "Always on some kid shit."

"That wasn't me," Kwame spoke up like a child being chastised by his mother.

Julian threw his hands in the air, "Rome did it."

"What?!" Roman whipped his head at Julian and growled lowly. "You ain't shit, bro."

"We covered that base already, Banana in Pajamas," Kwame grunted, letting Julian go. "Rome, you better clean that shit up. Can't take y'all nowhere without breaking something."

"This is exactly why you aren't allowed in my house," Brielle grunted, walking away.

Roman followed Wren inside of the house. "Let me help you with that."

"Roman," Wren gritted her teeth. "You have done enough. Get away from me."

"I didn't do it," Roman found himself getting irritated with defending himself to her. It's been months since he'd spoken to her and this is not how he imagined this going.

Wren turned around to face him with a stern look on her face. She stared at him intently for a few moments before her expression softened and she took a step back. "It doesn't matter, Roman. It's over."

She walked away, leaving Roman alone to pick up his face off the floor. Running his hand down his face, he fished his keys out of his pocket and left. He might've lost the battle, but he was not going to lose the war. He had a stake on Wren's heart and come hell or high water, he was coming to collect.

Wren Franklin

Wren stood in the middle of Kwame's guest bedroom and sighed to herself after tucking her hair behind her ears. There was a reason she avoided Roman like the plague. She wasn't fully over him. He'd find every chance he could to bombard her with reasons why they needed to be together or statements she knew he would later flake on. All in all, she was tired. She wanted something new to distract her from that old thing.

Roman may have had her heart but his lease was up, and it was time to give it back.

A soft knock on the door prompted her to wipe her tears and straighten her demeanor.

Brielle stepped in and smiled. "Are you okay?"

Wren forced a smile and laughed her encounter with Roman off, as if it were nothing and he was nothing to her. "Yeah, why wouldn't I be? It's just beer. The cleaners can get it out."

"Wren," Brielle hummed looking over her. "You know, if you don't deal with this now, you're evidently going to break."

"What is there to deal with, Bri? It's done. There isn't any going back. I'm moving forward. If I don't, then I'm stuck."

"But—"

"But, nothing! Roman had his time. Now, it's up, Wren needs love, too, and she's going to get it."

It was like a flashback for Brielle all over again. A lesson learned the hard way and she only hoped that Wren learned it from her and wouldn't have to go through it on her own. "Just don't sell yourself short."

"Never no more."

With that, Wren straightened herself up and headed out the door. "I'll see y'all later. I'm going home, I have had enough fun for a day."

After they hugged each other, Wren floated out the house with tears in her eyes. Getting over Roman was harder than she wanted it to be. He left an imprint on her soul and she wanted it gone.

ren Franklin

EXAMINING HERSELF IN THE FULL-LENGTH MIRROR, she smirked at her reflection. This was her first date, in months, and it was nice just to get out of the house for a change of scenery. Now that Kwame was completely settled into his new home and back in the city without needing her help, she was going to enjoy herself. That started with meeting Henry at La Boheme. Henry Taylor was a new real estate broker in the area that she'd had the privilege of talking to at a few open houses and property tours. Every time she saw him, he was always nice and complimented her. Wren lived for self-assurance and Henry had definitely given her that.

It seemed like the more attention she received, the more she flourished. All of that stemmed from her father being in and out of her life. He was just as inconsistent as Roman, so there was no wonder that she was taken by him. Hopefully, tonight, she could push the thoughts of men and their inconsistent ways to the back of her mind while she got lost in Henry. Well, that was the hope anyway. Henry's stature alone would make any woman stop in their tracks and do a double take. He was six feet even and looked like he floated off the pages of GQ. His cognac-colored eyes danced under his bushy brows. His jawline was tight and chiseled. Henry was the type of man that made you grunt and bite your lip when you examined him from head to toe. His caramel skin was smooth and his smile was priceless. It was no wonder why Wren jumped at the opportunity when it was presented to her. Any chance to see what Henry Taylor was made out of was always a good idea.

She tossed her hair over her shoulder and smirked one last time in approval of her soft butter cream dress against her chocolate skin, before grabbing her keys and heading out of the door. When she got to the restaurant, she stood in the foyer, scanning the area for Henry. Adjusting the hem of her dress, after she spotted him, she coolly strolled over to him.

"Hey, Henry," she beamed, opening her arms for a hug. Not only did he not stand to his feet to greet her, but he was engaged in a conversation on his phone. Holding his finger up for Wren to hold on, he continued his conversation. Wren pushed her eyebrows together and looked around oddly before dropping her arms and taking her seat. "Or not."

A few minutes later, Henry hung up and smiled apologetically at her. "I'm so sorry. I have a couple who keeps changing their mind and it's been draining. How are you?"

Wren was already put off and his inability to be a gentleman for five minutes rubbed her the wrong way.

"Hmm," Wren raised her brow and nodded slowly

before she even considered answering the question. Her right mind was telling her to order some food to go, make him pay for it and see herself out. "I'm okay."

"Have you ever eaten here?" Henry asked, looking around. "I'm not used to places with white tablecloths."

Wren pinned her brows together and tilted her head to the side slightly and squinted. "As opposed to...?"

"You know what I mean. I mean, I usually don't take women to fancy restaurants on the first date. Especially if I don't know if they're putting out or not." Wren was taken aback by Henry's forwardness surrounding the date he asked her on. "You've been on several, you know how it goes."

"Actually," she scoffed slightly and shook her head before chuckling. "I have no idea what you mean by that. But I'll let it go."

"You look nice," the more Henry talked, the more her skin crawled. Who was this man and where did he come from? She wanted him to go back to the guy she'd been gawking over for the last couple of weeks. It was painful how clear it was becoming this was a waste of her time.

Wren flipped her hair across her shoulder and winced. "Thank you."

"So, what made you agree to have dinner with me?" Henry's self-assuredness had gone from sexy to downright nauseating.

Wren smiled politely as the waitress approached the table. Wren's mind was made up and she wasn't going to sit through this much longer. She had no business being here with him and she knew it. Henry's persona was sickening. "Hi, I'm Jas—"

"Let me get a uhhhhh... Some crown. How much does

that cost?" Henry looked at the waitress, but his eyes didn't leave her breast.

Wren's facial expression became more twisted as Henry went on about the cost of Crown, with or without water. "The lady will have a water with lemon."

"I'm actually okay. Don't worry about me."

"Are you sure?"

"Very," Wren nodded her head, now trying to figure out her best exit strategy. This date was going nowhere fast. It was like watching a train wreck.

Henry's smirk made her itch. "You don't think you should hydrate?"

"Drank a lot of water during the day." Looking around, she tried to think of all the ways to salvage this date, but there were none. Hope for Henry had dwindled down to the lowest of flames and it didn't even flicker. One thing she knew for sure was that if she didn't get out of here soon, he was going to start tap dancing on her nerves.

The waitress returned shortly after disappearing with Henry's Crown and water. This was the perfect time for Wren to make her exit. She couldn't sit still a minute longer with him. As hungry as she was, she wasn't even considering breaking bread with him, especially after learning he was only here for one thing.

Wren narrowed her eyes and read the name tag pinned on the waitress' crisp white blouse and smiled. "Jasmoné... that is a beautiful name. Listen, I'm going to go ahead and tip you for holding up a table."

Henry jerked his neck back and looked at her oddly, as she pushed herself away from the table and handed the waitress a few twenty-dollar bills. "You're leaving? Come on. Sit your pretty ass down and let's finish dinner and then you know... a couple of rounds at your place."

"You know," she smiled, softly pushing the hair out of her face. "I can't do this. I'm not the right fit for you. And, before I waste any more of your time, I'm going to see myself out. You enjoy yourself. Do you need me to cover your drink or you got it?"

Before he could answer her, she turned on her heels and strutted out of the restaurant. Climbing into her car, she groaned at her stomach growling. Wren needed to unload this awful date and eat and there was nowhere better to do that than with Nadia.

"Yes, my love," Nadia's voice flowed through the car after Wren's call connected. "How was the date with Henry?"

"Girl," Wren smacked her lips and rolled her eyes. "Where are you?"

"At the house, drinking wine and looking over the layout for the restaurant. Are you hungry?"

"How did you know?"

"Wild guess. Use your key, I'll see you soon."

Disconnecting the call, Wren made her way over to Nadia's house. Pulling into the driveway, she took a minute to inhale and release while looking around at Nadia's cute Los Angeles home. It was big enough for her and she made it her happy place. Wren appreciated that she was always considered first for her family and friends' property searches. Kwame even cut her in on the property deal for Isabella's new restaurant. After the success of the first restaurant it Isabella's business took off like a rocket. They were moving up in their careers and kept her pockets lined nicely, too.

Wren slowly walked into the house and inhaled the scent of basil, garlic and seafood. A smile instantly crossed her face as she closed the door behind her. "What man did you have in here? Cooking like this only means one thing."

Wren helped herself in the kitchen and started picking through the pot on the stove. Angel hair pasta in white wine clam sauce, with pesto, crab meat, shrimp and mussels was Nadia's signature dish and Wren's mouth watered.

"Girl," Nadia chuckled, moving her away from the stove with her hip. "You know better. No men in my house, let alone men, period. Go, sit down. I got it."

"Why are you so good to me?" Wren cooed, sitting at the oak farm yard table. She admired how Nadia's home was set up like there was a family living here. When Nadia started decorating her house, she was set on making it feel like the home she never had. When you walked in, she wanted you greeted by a home-cooked meal, warm hues of paint on the walls and a subtle hint of vanilla and lemon lingering in the fabrics. She'd done a great job of doing it, too. Wren found herself crashing in Nadia's guest room after long nights of work.

"Eh," Nadia chuckled with a smile as she fixed a plate for Wren and herself. "I kind of love you."

"Kind of? You know I'm like the little sister you never had."

"You are so right about that," Nadia placed the plates on the table and walked across the kitchen for the bottle of wine and glasses. "Spill the tea."

Wren didn't even wait for Nadia to join her at the table before she started eating. "Where do you want me to start?"

"The minute you hesitated on leaving and didn't." Filling the glasses of wine, Nadia sat down.

"So, I walk in and this negro didn't even stand up to greet me. He held up his finger and continued his phone call. Then, he said some shit about not taking women to restaurants with white tablecloths on the first date unless he knew that they were putting out. And when the waitress came to take our drink orders, this cheap ass bastard orders me water."

"Had you waited around for dinner, he would've ordered you a side salad," Nadia chuckled into her glass of wine. "Everything that glitters ain't always gold, baby. Sometimes it's gold plated nickel. The shit that, once you put it on, it's going to cause a nasty rash and turn your neck green."

"I'm happy I didn't waste a year of my life to find that out," Wren exhaled, shaking the thought of Roman out of her mind.

Nadia picked up on it but remained silent. She pushed Brielle to go out and live her best life and saw how that ended up. So, this time around, she was going to mind her business and drink her wine.

"Nadia, I swear I am not supposed to be dating." Wren placed her hand on her head and groaned. "I clearly suck at it."

"It's not you that sucks. It's your decision-making skills that suck."

Wren cut her eyes over at Nadia, who shrugged her shoulders. "All I'm saying, Wren, is turn off the part of you that needs reassurance and start looking at these men without your rose-colored glasses. They are going to show you exactly what you want to see. Your job is to find out if it's bullshit or not."

"Why do you always have to make sense?"

"Someone has to," Nadia smirked. "Maybe, right now isn't your time. Maybe you should just enjoy being solo. Date yourself and reset your standards."

"Thank you."

"Don't thank me, baby. Charge it to your tab. One day, I'm going to need you in the same capacity."

Two bottles of wine later, Wren ended up in the guest room, knocked out in the middle of the bed. Nadia only hoped that everything she'd told her set in and resonated with Wren. She was far too good to be wasting her time with men who didn't know how to be a man.

3

 oman Daniels

It was almost three in the morning and Roman was awakened out of a dead sleep by his phone ringing. Initially, he thought that he could ignore it but, the longer he refused to answer, the more persistent the caller was. He groaned and reached over to the nightstand and grabbed the source of his annoyance. Tiredly, he placed the phone to his ear, not bothering to see who it was. There was only one person in the whole world who didn't care what time they called him and that was his mother. Her timing didn't wait on the sun at all. She would call just to chat and, other times, to scream about his sister.

"Yeah, ma," Roman's voice was heavy and exhausted. "What's up?"

"Your fast ass sister just waltzed her ass back in this house. She's been gone for two days, playing house with that boy and had the nerve to come back in here like she

23

pays rent! I've been texting and calling her, and do you think she's had the common decency to reply? Let me know she was alive? Hell, she could've sent me a smoke signal or something. I'm telling you, right damn now, Roman, you better come and get her," his mother fired off without taking a breath.

Grudgingly, he sat on the edge of the bed and ran his hand down his face. "Where has she been for two days?"

"With that dope dealing boy."

"Mama, don't tell him that," Kamaiyah's voice was faint in the background but Roman could pick up on the fear she had. The fear of Roman finding out that she was doing something she had no business doing. "You know he's going to come down here and cause a scene."

"You damn right I'm going to cause a scene," Roman muttered under his voice.

"Kamaiyah, get your little ass away from me, right now, before I knock your head off your damn body." Roman groaned, listening to the two of them go back and forth. He knew that sleep was far from him. Swinging his arms aggressively in the air, he pushed himself out of the bed and found a t-shirt and shorts to put on.

"I'm on my way."

"She'll be packed up by the time you get here. I'm not doing this shit no more." A few more words were shared between his mother and Kamaiyah before he hung up and groaned heavily. Walking out of his condo, he jogged down the stairs and headed toward Compton.

The drive was longer than usual, due to the fact that Roman didn't want to be anywhere near the drama of Kamaiyah and her inability to listen. He had to be both a brother and a father to her and his biggest fear was that she would get caught up with some boy from around the way.

He was facing that head-on and it was unsettling. Their mother had done everything she could possibly do when it came to raising them, but she was tired and Roman knew it.

Finally reaching Compton, he crept through his old neighborhood and shook his head at the sight. Corner boys and gang bangers, bars over windows and injustice police patrol made him cringe. He hated it all. If it took removing Kamaiyah from this environment to get her head on straight, then that's what he would have to do. She wouldn't be impeding on anything important. Roman's life consisted of work and home. Since Wren walked out of his life, he was in no rush to entertain anyone else, especially if it wasn't her. He'd seen her only in passing. She made a point not to be at group events if he was going to be there. And if he did, it was always for a few minutes before she would find a reason to leave.

The knock on his window broke him out of his thoughts. Realizing he'd been daydreaming at the stop sign, he groaned before looking over his shoulder at the hooded man at his driver's side. Roman hadn't been back to Compton in some time but he knew the deal. After Senior died, Roman wanted to be just like him, even if that meant defying his mother's law and getting down with the gang. Because of the weight of Senior's name, the gang protected him and his family. But this wasn't back in the day and, lately, the young bloods had no respect for the ones who proceeded them. Roman grabbed his gun from between the seat and his flag out the center console and draped it on his lap. The flag was a representation of where he came from and what he would never return to. He always had to stay strapped when he came to Compton. Rolling his window down, he looked the man over.

"What's good, blood? Who you here to see?" Roman

couldn't help but laugh. He smirked and took his flag off his lap and laid it on the steering wheel.

"You know, back in the day, you used to know who the homies were. You haven't been out here long enough to see some shit. Get the fuck away from my car, blood."

Out the corner of his eye, he saw a few more guys approach his car. Growling lowly, he pushed his door open and hopped out.

"Do we have a problem?" The voice bellowed over the crowd of young boys surrounding Roman's car. Roman knew that voice from anywhere. Its roughness was distinct, and he could pick it up without an issue.

Ronnie.

Ronnie was an OG that used to move around the city with his pops before he was shot and killed. Ronnie made sure that his mom had everything she needed but she detested Ronnie and the gang over Senior's death. But that never stopped Ronnie from doing what was right by her. For that reason alone, Roman had great respect for him. He might've resented growing up here, but he would never resent the gems that he planted in his spirit.

"I asked him who he was," the hooded man admitted, looking back at his back up, which started to disburse now that Ronnie had emerged.

"This is Piru. We don't care about your baby ass flag, nigga. Don't nobody know you, blood." Roman kissed his teeth at that comment and shook his head. It would be easy to revert back to his old ways, but he now had too much to lose.

He groaned in annoyance while his eyes started scanning the area. Finally spotting Ronnie move in closer through the sea of people parting to make way for him to walk through. "Ronnie, get these niggas out of my face, man."

"Ro!" Ronnie greeted, breaking through the crowd. "You don't come through the hood no more. Don't be mad at the homies for not knowing who you are."

Roman shook his head at Ronnie's comment and relaxed his stance slightly. Looking back over the remaining crowd, Ronnie nodded their way. "He's good, he's family."

Greeting Ronnie with their handshake, Roman released a low sigh of relief after the group dispersed, leaving the two of them there. "You here to check in on Kamaiyah?"

He nodded his head, still taking in his surroundings. "Ain't no other reason for me to be here, Ro. You know who she been messing with?"

Ronnie kissed his teeth and ran his hand over the top of his head and chuckled. "Some mark ass nigga that wants to be down with Piru. That ain't the only reason you need to be around, though."

"You fucking with me?" Roman didn't take in anything past hearing that Kamaiyah was messing with someone who was unworthy of her time and attention.

"I look like I'm fucking with you, Ro? The baby girls always go after what their daddy was, and, in your case, her brother." Ronnie shared, leaning back on Roman's car. "Not to mention, niggas wouldn't dare step to her if you were doing what you were supposed to be doing around here."

"And what's that, Ronnie? Unifying a city that doesn't care if I live or die? If my pops lived or died? Man, please! These niggas don't respect nobody."

"You're wrong. They respected the fuck out of Senior. His name resonates with the people. They don't know who the fuck you are and that's on you. You got out of here and didn't look back. You making money, making moves and didn't even bother reaching back for none of us. That's fucked up and it's going to get your ass shot." Roman looked over at Ronnie for a few seconds before responding. He didn't have any words because Ronnie was right. Roman didn't even want to come to get his sister. But, if he didn't, he was running the risk of his sister being left on the streets.

Roman kissed his teeth once more and spotted the police creeping around the corner, looking for trouble to get into. "I'm going to get out of here. Stay up."

"You, too. Don't get your ass caught up in anything. Call me if some shit needs to go down. You got too much to lose," Ronnie responded, taking a step back and smirking. "Proud of you, little nigga. Tell Shelia I asked about her."

"Thank you. You know Shelia ain't looking for you."

"Don't matter. We family around here, like it or not."

Continuing his pursuit to his mother's house, he parked his car on the curb and put both his flag and gun away before getting out. Walking up the uneven sidewalk to the house, he could hear the fussing from the front door. "You got to be kidding me."

Using his key, he let himself in to see Kamaiyah's bags packed by the front door and the two of them fussing in the hallway. Nothing about home had changed, down to the cigarette burning in the ashtray. Shelia rarely smoked but, when she was stressed out, it burned like incense at an Erykah Badu concert.

"Kamaiyah," his voice bellowed down the hall. "Get your ass in here, girl."

"Oh, look. Your brother is here. Tell him what you just told me."

"Ma, the whole damn block can hear you," Roman groaned, rubbing his head. "Cool your ass out."

She stopped and whipped her head around. "Boy, I look

like I care about the whole damn block? The whole damn block knows she's been running around like she lost her damn mind."

"Okay," Roman spoke up trying to create some peace. He loathed when she got like this. Not just because of her health but she was liable to do something drastic. "That's enough, ma. I'll take her for the rest of the school year and then we'll figure out what's going on for the summer."

"Roman, I'm telling you. Keeping you and your daddy off the streets was hard enough, I am not about to be raising no baby."

"Before you say anything, no, I'm not pregnant," Kamaiyah mumbled, avoiding Roman's glare of disappointment.

Roman sat down and put the cigarette out and looked at Kamaiyah cowering in the hallway. "Go get in the car, Kamaiyah. I'll bring your bags out in a minute."

She inched past Shelia before scurrying off to the car. With a heavy sigh, Roman looked at his mother and examined her body language. "You need to calm your ass down before you give yourself another heart attack."

"You got to watch after her. I can't keep doing this. I am tired and she is a damn handful. She thinks she knows everything."

"So, I guess I'm on daddy duty again," Roman shook his head and sat up. "I already told you to move out of this hellhole."

"Where the hell am I going, Roman? I'm not moving out of my city to be bougie in the hills."

"Ma, all of those are excuses not to leave. I already told you, I will get you a house. The longer she's in this environment, the more she's liable to become a product of it."

"Like you, Piru?"

The only reason Roman came home was because of Kamaiyah, the reason he left was because of his mother. He loved her, he wanted more for her, but she had to want it, too. "Don't bring it up. It is what it is."

"You sound like your damn daddy," Shelia scoffed and placed her hands on her hips. "Just like him."

Roman couldn't stand the comparison to Senior. He wasn't Senior and he was unsure of whether he could ever fill the shoes he left behind.

"Are you taking her or what? The next step is kicking her the hell out."

"Ma, why? When has that ever worked for you?" Roman watched as Shelia's eyes squinted at him. "You kicked pops out, three days later he was gone. You put me out, I went searching for a home and found it on the streets. Kamaiyah ain't built like the rest of us."

He took a minute to pause and reset his bubbling resentment. At the end of the day, he was just as responsible for Kamaiyah as she was. That's what Senior would've wanted. "Listen, I got it. Don't worry about none of it."

Pushing himself off the couch, he kissed her cheek and stalked toward the door to pick up Kamaiyah's things. "Love you, Ma."

oman Daniels

HEADING OUT OF COMPTON, ROMAN GRIPPED THE steering wheel and went back and forth with himself on where to start their conversation. There were a million things going through his mind, with Ronnie's conversation resting heavily at the forefront. He didn't know where to start or how to approach her, how to provide what she needed or how to be her big brother.

"You might as well just say it," Kamaiyah groaned looking at the street lights as they rode past them. "Tell me how much of a disappointment I am."

"K," Roman started, then stopped to settle the nerve that she unknowingly hit. "K, why would you even say that?"

"Because I hear it all damn day. How much of a disappointment I am to her; how much I'm going to be a stereotype because I can't stay out of trouble. I get sick of hearing that shit."

Roman sucked in a deep breath, as he approached the stop light. "I'm not making no excuses for ma, but she hasn't been the same since Senior died."

"And how is that my fault? I'm not the reason he was killed."

"No, you weren't. It's no one's fault. She was never taught how to grieve and to heal properly. If you look around, everyone is like that in Compton. I understand you're frustrated but that doesn't warrant you to run around these streets with some nigga that does not have your best interest in mind."

"Here you go."

"You're damn right, here I go," Roman based, pulling off from the light. "These niggas don't love you, Maiyah. They want pussy and someone to hold their weed. These streets ain't nowhere for you to be."

"But it was somewhere for you to be?"

Pinching the bridge of his nose, he let out a pensive groan before looking at her. "You and mom with that bull-shit. I swear, y'all be irking my damn nerves with that. I did what I had to do to survive and when I found an out, I took that shit. I want the best for you, and it's not in the streets."

She huffed and folded her arms across her chest. "You and Senior were the only men I had to look up to. He got shot and killed by someone he knew, and you high tailed it out of there the minute you could. So, forgive me if I'm a little irritated by this."

"You need to cool your little irritated ass off, K. You're seventeen, you're not grown. Just because you don't like the way things are going don't mean you can do what the hell you want, thinking it's going to yield the results you want. That ain't it, baby girl."

"You're not my daddy, Rome."

"I'm the closest damn thing you got to one. So, shut the hell up and listen," Roman's irritation had turned up a notch and the bass in his voice caused Kamaiyah to jump slightly in her seat. "Senior is rolling in his damn grave. This is the last thing he wanted for you. To get caught up in some lame ass wannabe nigga. Whatever trouble you might be in better not find its way to my doorstep."

Silence fell between them as Roman continued to his house. All the hopes he had of getting some sleep when he returned were fleeting. "You and dad were the only examples I had. Of course, I was going to be like my mother and follow in her footsteps. What girl doesn't want to be sought out by the guy everyone knows?"

He couldn't argue with her because she was right. "I thought that was the guy I was supposed to go after. The guy that left you hanging, getting into fights over him, disappearing for days and then popping up. It's like I say I won't do what mom did, but I found myself taking back everything because of him. That's what I saw you, mommy and Senior do."

Kamaiyah's words rang over and over in Roman's head. His chest tightened and his mouth got dry. It hit him like a ton of bricks to hear the truth he knew deep down but couldn't bring himself to say out loud.

Pulling into the parking lot of his building, he looked over at her and put the car in park. "I need you to know, I'm sorry. I didn't know you were watching me."

"Ro, you're my big brother, you're damn near my daddy. Why wouldn't I watch you? I might've been quiet, but I was watching everything you did."

"Yeah, now I got to unteach everything you learned. Come on."

Once Kamaiyah was settled in the guest room, Roman shuffled into his room and sat down on the edge of the bed with his phone in his hand. Everything in him wanted to call Wren and apologize for making a mess of everything. But, more than anything, he longed to hear her voice. Feel her touch. Inhale her sweet scent. He missed her more than he had the words to express. Falling back on the bed, he stared at the ceiling before he dozed off to sleep.

"Boy, you look like hell," Kwame pointed out the bags underneath Roman's eyes before he flipped a middle finger in his direction. "Oh, Papi, you're a little too short for me."

"You're stupid," Julian chuckled, bouncing the basketball and taking a shot.

The three of them stood in the middle of the basketball court shooting around, unloading their week and blowing off steam. Since Julian and Brielle were back on the same page of the same book, it seemed like the pull between the group had died down. Julian was making a lot more time for the family instead of hanging out, which they all understood. They urged Julian to take care of home before he did anything else. Kwame was still up to no good while Roman was trying to settle with who he was and get everything back on track.

Roman shook his head at Kwame's banter and sat down on the bench. "I appreciate your letting me down so easily."

"What's good?" Julian asked, taking a swig from his water bottle. "You look all tense."

"Kamaiyah got kicked out by mom dukes last night... Well, this morning. I had to drive my ass to Compton before the crack of dawn's ass. Almost got shot by my own set and had to listen to my mom lose her damn mind. And, to top this all off, Kamaiyah's ass got caught up with some nigga. She hasn't told me all the details but I'm sure that it's better for her to be here than there."

"Damn," Julian grunted, running his hand over his fresh fade. "The whole point of getting out the hood is never having to go back. Why is mom dukes still there? She should've been out the minute you could get them out."

"She has a million excuses why she doesn't want to go but it's really because that's where Senior is buried. She might hate him for leaving her, but she is not going too far away from him. Plus, the OGs got her. Doesn't matter if she's here or there, she's good."

Kwame propped his leg up on the bench and rested his elbows on his knee. "That's heavy. I can't tell you the last time I've been to Watts..."

Roman leaned back and looked out into the distance. "I'm not going back. Last night exposed a part of my life I've tried my damnedest to separate myself from. It broke my heart to hear that her decisions were molded by who I used to be and who Senior was. My own sister has no clue who I am now."

"What are you going to do about it?" Julian asked, looking over Roman's bothered demeanor.

"I just got to step up to the plate and be the man Senior would've wanted me to be." Roman shrugged his shoulders. The thought of Wren was floating around in his mind since the early morning. "The man *she* wanted me to be."

"Listen, Wren don't want your ass," Kwame snickered. "Lower your standards, my man."

 ren Franklin

AFTER THE HORRIBLE DATE SHE COULDN'T SIT THROUGH the other night, Wren needed to figure out where her bad decisions stemmed from. And, like every other woman with men issues, the root of it always lie with someone they knew. For Wren, all her issues of self-worth and reassurance lie in the hands of her father. Whether he knew it or not, his inability to stay put caused a ripple effect in her own life. She went after men who were emotionally unavailable to love her or men who only saw her as an object. It had now become exhausting and she needed to look at the cause of her frustrations in the face.

She pulled into the driveway of her father's Baldwin Hills home and threw the car in park. Recently, he'd decided that it was time to settle down and share his life with someone. Wren always found that mentality aggravating. Terry had run through a slew of women who were willing and ready to give their hearts to him, but he claimed that he wasn't ready. It never stopped him from having kids with them and moving on to the next woman ready to bend over backwards for him.

Using her key to let herself in, she was hit with the aroma of tacos. "Hey!"

"Hey, baby girl," Terry's voice bellowed from the kitchen into the small foyer of the house. Closing the door behind her, she proceeded to the kitchen to see him placing all the food on the countertops. One thing Terry loved to do was cook. Kwame must've picked up this skill, too. They used it to keep women eating out the palms of their hands.

He turned around to hug Wren and kiss the top of her head. Their relationship was still fresh. When Terry met his wife, Farrah, he decided it was time to be in the lives of the children he fathered, full-time. Some weren't as willing as Wren and Kwame were but that was their battle and not hers to fight. "Where's Nadia?"

"She'll be here. You know she doesn't ever miss a taco night," Wren chuckled before traveling to the refrigerator from the island to grab a bottle of water. "Where is Farrah?"

"She ran to the store to get limes for the margaritas. You know how y'all do when you get together," he chuckled lightly, noticing the discomfort on his daughter's face. "What's going on with you? How's work?"

"Good," she shrugged before taking and seat and plowing her hair out of her face. "As good as it can be. I probably complicated a working relationship, but I'll be cool."

"You went on a date with him?"

"I did and it was terrible," Wren rested her palm on her cheek and shook her head, trying to shake off the memory of it. "It's like the guys either can't love me back or they want their way and leave."

Folding her arms on the table, she looked at her father and pushed her eyebrows together. "Why are you looking at me like it's my fault?"

"Because it is, Terry."

He chuckled softly and wiped his wet hands on the towel before throwing it on the counter and joining her at the table. "How is it my fault?"

Terry knew his absence from his children's lives had an everlasting effect on them. Especially Wren, who seemed to need a lot more guidance from him than the rest of them. He braced himself as Wren pursed her lips together and focused on the lines in his face.

She inhaled and released the air from her lungs a few seconds afterward. "You never taught me what I should've been looking for in a man. Because of that, I looked everywhere for assurance and validation. I looked for you in the hearts of damn near every man I involved myself with. It took me breaking up with Roman to see that maybe, this whole time, it was something wrong with me. Maybe I was expecting too much."

Terry knew, without a shadow of a doubt, that the blame solely lie with him as much as the healing did. "You were expecting to be loved back. I know you don't want to hear this but, in Roman's case, I get the feeling that he loved you, he just wasn't sure how to return the love you gave. You are like your mother in a lot of ways."

"It's funny to me that you know how my mother loved you and yet you were running around everywhere else."

"Touché," Terry chuckled, leaning back in the wooden chair. "The women I cared about, I remember vividly. Your mother and Kwame's mother are the reason you two are so close. If it wasn't for the vast amount of love they held for me, you two wouldn't know each other."

"Hmm," Wren hummed, listening to what he had to say.

He stroked his beard and looked away for a moment. "I admit that I wasn't the best man I could be. And not to make excuses, but I was Crenshaw through and through. Hell, I still am. I chose exactly who I wanted to be and I paid for that dearly. Being a player, to me, was better than gang banging and being dead before twenty. Looking back on it, I caused the same amount of damage to you that my father did to me."

When Terry started his storytelling, Wren turned off everything else in her mind to focus on what he was saying. He always had some wisdom to share, whether she wanted to hear it or not. "I could be wrong but Roman could be the same guy I was at his age. Too damn scared to give the love back. It was never a secret that I loved your mother. She was probably the best thing to ever happen to me, then. But she was too damn good for me. That, alone, would make any man who isn't sure about who he is, step back. I fell back and, by the time I looked up to grab her again, she was gone."

"It's funny to me that you guys can't realize that at the moment. We got to leave for you to get it."

"Wren, be honest. If he were to realize that when you demanded it, would you have believed him? Would you have wanted to continue on with him and without thinking about the what ifs?"

Wren broke eye contact with him and looked away. "I'm back."

Farrah walked in just in time for her to quickly shift the mood. "Hey, Wren. You look pretty."

After greeting Farrah with a hug, she took the bags from her hands and placed them on the counter. "Thank you. What did I walk into?"

Farrah's eyes shifted from Wren to Terry, who still sat at the table, waiting for Wren to rejoin him. "Baby girl was telling me that I'm the reason she chooses the men she does."

Farrah scoffed and looked over at Terry. "You are."

"Damn," he whistled. "I have no backup, do I?"

"None at all. But we talked about this. She's only going to go after what you've taught her to go after."

"And then he asked if I would've believed Roman if he said he loved him when I demanded to know," Wren added, unpacking all the contents needed to make a margarita.

Farrah turned to watch Wren begin to make a margarita for the both of them. "Well, would you have?"

"No," Wren muttered to herself before taking a shot of tequila, then poured some into the mixer. "I wouldn't have. I would've thought he said it just to appease me."

"So, at this very moment what do you want? Do you want him back or do you want to move on?"

"I don't know... I want to figure out me."

Farrah clasped her hands together and smiled at Wren. "There's a start."

"See? Easy fix," Terry announced standing up.

"Not so fast, babe," Farrah held her hand up. "This doesn't let you off the hook of being a father to your daughter. You have to be the man she needs. I think you should take her on a few dates."

Wren smirked, trying her best to hide the smile that was creeping across her face. "You owe me a couple daddy-daughter dances and ice cream dates."

Terry beamed at the two and nodded his head. "You got

it. Tell me when and I'll come and pick you up and show you a good time."

"Good, let's eat."

ROMAN DANIELS

THE DAY HAD GOTTEN AWAY FROM HIM. INSTEAD OF heading into the shop to see how the few custom orders were coming along, he decided to get Kamaiyah ready for her new school. Switching schools in the middle of the school year wasn't ideal but, due to her situation, it was necessary. Roman wanted to make sure that she was more than comfortable to start school on Monday.

"Maiyah, come here," Roman's voice bellowed from the kitchen. "Sit down. We need to have a real talk before I head over to the shop."

Placing the rest of the bags in her room, she walked down the hall and joined Roman in the kitchen. "What's up?"

"I know that you aren't thrilled to be here and that's fine. I want you safe and comfortable and I will do everything in my power to assure that you are. But you got to be real with me. I will go hand over fist and to war for you every time. But if you don't let me in on what's going on in your head and on that phone, and I have to find out some off the wall type of way, I'm going to lose my shit. You have a curfew; you will be in this house by eight on the weekdays and nine on the weekends, unless you're out with me. Your narrow ass will be in school every day. If I find out otherwise, it's my foot in your ass. Understand?"

Kamaiyah's disgruntled expression gave off the feeling

that she wasn't going to adhere to anything Roman had said. "Am I in prison or something?"

"Do you want to go there?" Roman asked, raising his brows. "Because I can let you go back home with that dumbass boy who will sell you out for a slap on the wrist."

Kamaiyah's eyesr bulged out her head slightly as Roman shrugged his shoulders. "You thought that I wasn't going to figure out what the hell you been up to?"

"Shelia snitched on me?" Kamaiyah asked in disbelief, making Roman drop his head and chuckle lowly.

"Kamaiyah, you aren't taking any of this shit seriously. You better be happy she told me. That's beside the point. The point is that I'm not taking any bullshit off of you whatsoever. I have pulled a lot of strings and asked for a lot of favors to get your ungrateful ass in the best school in the area." Roman popped the top of a bottle of water and watched as Kamaiyah chewed on the rules he laid down. "Don't think about how to get around them either. You think you're slicker than a can of oil, you ain't. I'm slicker than Senior's hair used to be. Don't even think about playing me."

"Don't nobody want to play you, Rome," Kamaiyah kissed her teeth and started walking down the hall.

"I would hate to put my foot up your ass over some bullshit!" he shouted behind her before hearing her room door slam. "I'll take that bitch off the hinges! Keep it up, youngblood!"

Pressing his back against the wall, he groaned and palmed his face. Kamaiyah was going to test every ounce of gangsta he had left in him. She was going to be the sole reason that Roman found himself in a mugshot with a smile on his face.

He wanted to be her big brother but Kamaiyah needed

a father. That was something she never had the pleasure of experiencing in its entirety. He was trying to balance being both, especially when he hadn't had the pleasure either. After leaving forty dollars on the counter for her to order a pizza, he left and drove down to his shop.

Roman owned a body shop that specialized in custom cars. Every car was different and Roman had a personal touch on every one of them. He got enough of hotwiring cars in the hood and decided to go to school for business. He was proud to say that he made it out and made something of himself. He wanted Kamaiyah to feel this same sense of pride he felt. But she had to want to do the right thing just as much as he wanted her to do it.

Between the thoughts of Wren and Kamaiyah, he needed this time. Just him in the shop with paint and a design was all he needed to center himself and look ahead to the future. He saw it vividly: Wren by his side again, permanently, and Kamaiyah safe and flourishing. While he worked, he whispered a silent prayer to himself.

Dear God, know my heart. I need this. I need her. Amen.

$\mathcal{N}$adia Garrett

HER PERFECTLY SCULPTED EYEBROWS PINCHED SO closely together they were soon going to fuse themselves into one another. Her wide eyes were now as chinky as they could get as she squinted them in ultimate aggravation. She peered across the table at Kwame, trying her best not to flip the table and put her hands on him. Nadia knew that working with Kwame was going to upset her peace, but she never thought that he could piss her off this much.

His smug smirk was going to be the reason he would have to walk around with shades on to cover the purple rings around his eyes. Kwame operated everything the same way he operated his life: hastily and rough while Nadia liked to take her time, especially with the details. Opening Isabella's third restaurant was causing more stress to their already strained relationship, or a lack thereof, than it should've.

Nadia closed her binder and clamped down on her lip as hard as she could to avoid saying anything out the way to him. It wasn't out of respect; it was based on her trying to collect the rest of her peace that she could. But Kwame wasn't going to let her walk away from him without hitting the red button of her aggravation. "Why can't you just stop being a damn pain in my ass and do what I tell you to do?"

"What you *tell* me to do?" she stopped what she was doing and took the bait. "Tell me..." The tip of her tongue traced her bottom lip as she contemplated telling him where to go and how fast he could get there. "First of all, nigga..."

"Damn, black on black hate," Kwame stood up from the table and looked over her body, cloaked in pure irritation.

Nadia pinched the bridge on her nose and resumed picking her things up and placing them into her bag. After a second thought, she stopped and looked at him. "The more I work with you, the more I want to bash your head into a fucking wall. What you won't ever do in your pathetic ass life is tell me what to do. I am more than capable of thinking for me and you."

"Nadia, you seem to forget that I'm funding this restaurant and the other two," Kwame announced, as though it was going to make her back off. It wasn't. It only gave her more ammunition to dig further into him and make him feel as small as she could.

"Kwame, you seem to forget that I don't give a fuck and the first two were opened without any help from you. We are so off budget because you handle business like you handle your whores," Nadia pointed her manicured finger at him and forcefully spoke like she was six foot seven and weighed three hundred pounds.

Kwame's smirk turned into a lopsided grin as he stepped into her space. "Would you like to find out?"

Nadia growled and pushed him away from her. Gathering her things again, she turned on her heels and walked out of his office. Kwame leaned on the threshold of his office door and watched as she stormed away from him. He'd done this several times and always got the same result from her. Nadia's ability to strengthen her guard around him always failed when he entered her space. She had never come across a soul that she wanted to embrace and kill at the same time.

On her pursuit out his office building, down to her car, she glanced at her watch and groaned. She was late for taco night. Before she reached Baldwin Hills, she needed to relax her nerves as much as she could before she walked through the door. Wren's father could pick up on everything and she wanted to give no clue to anyone that Kwame had her ten types of fucked up.

Rolling the windows down to let the heat out of her car, she pulled out the parking garage and headed toward Crenshaw. Her music was loud, in an attempt to get her mind off of Kwame, but it failed her. Once she reached Terry's house, she killed the engine and powered her phone off. Everything that needed her attention could wait until later. Right now, she wanted tacos and tequila and not to think about anything else.

"I hope y'all left me some tacos," she spoke up loud enough to be heard over the laughs. Shuffling into the kitchen, Farrah stood up once she laid eyes on her. "Sorry, I'm late."

"I was wondering where you were," Wren spoke up with a mouth full of taco. Nadia cut her eyes over at her and rolled her eyes. "Oh. That's an attitude."

"My meeting ran over."

"Aren't you and Kwame working together on that

restaurant chain?" Farrah asked, motioning for Nadia to sit down.

Nadia sat across from Terry and pushed her tousled curls out of her face. "Mmhmm... He's working my damn nerves is what he's doing."

"Like father, like son," Farrah snickered, fixing Nadia a plate of tacos and a margarita.

Terry wiped his mouth with a napkin and shook his head. "I'm going to stop doing taco night if y'all keep ganging up on me like this."

"Y'all?" Nadia asked raising her brow. "I didn't do anything."

"Mhmm..." Terry cut his eyes lowly, enjoying how much his son had bothered Nadia prior to her arrival. "How many more restaurants do you two have left to do?"

"I was hoping that this was the last one, but we just got two more and we are so far over budget, it's ridiculous. But I don't want to talk about work. I just calmed down." Nadia groaned at the thought of Kwame she was trying to get out of her head. "What have y'all been talking about?"

Farrah placed the plate of tacos and the glass on the placemat in front of her. "Men."

"Oh, boy! Let me guess. Wren's date the other night?"

"Roman," Terry announced, smirking over his glass.

Nadia mirrored his smirk and looked at Wren. "There's a name I haven't had the pleasure of hearing in a while. Well, not in depth anyway."

"What we were talking about," Wren spoke up. "Were men who weren't ready to be in relationships who find creative ways to renege on a hand that they threw out."

"Everywhere you go, there's a basic ass man to make you rethink everything you thought you knew," Nadia muttered, taking a bite of her taco.

"Nadia, are you giving dating a shot yet?" Farrah asked as Nadia shook her head no. "Why not?"

"Why?" Nadia tucked her hair behind her ear and shrugged. "I'm not built for a relationship. I'm selfish. And because I know this, I do not go looking for a soul to corrupt."

"You just need the right man," Terry spoke up with Kwame in mind.

Nadia hummed and shook her head no. "I don't, because he doesn't exist."

"He exists, you're just picky as hell," Wren chuckled.

"I am not. I am reasonable and my standards are what they are. I will not relax them or lay them by the wayside because I want someone to hold me at night. That's crazy as hell," Nadia twisted her face in protest.

Farrah tilted her head to the side and hummed. "Where did you get those standards? Your parents?"

Nadia scoffed and began to laugh. "I guess you can say that. They showed me everything that I didn't want in a man and the type of woman I never wanted to be. Wren and I are different. She needs someone to love her because she has so much to give. The love she has to give is heavy. I'm not like that, at all. I don't need it."

"Everyone needs love, Nadia," Wren locked eyes with her.

"Why would I take a love that's going to hurt me? And why would I take the love I've found for myself and give it away without a second thought? I don't have enough to share. I have just enough to get me through."

"And who is for you can add to that," Terry added.

"And when we get men with baggage, who are just as broken as we are and they refuse to heal, are we supposed to take that little bit of love we have found for ourselves and hand it over to them? Why would I run the risk of never getting it back?" Nadia presented her question to Terry, who shifted his eyes over to Farrah.

"Because the love that is yours will knock you out and not only take from you but pour back into you. That's what you want, that's what all women deserve. Especially my girls."

Nadia nodded her head slowly before smirking. "Spoken like a true womanizer."

"That's it, no more taco night. You two are canceled," Terry huffed as Farrah, Nadia and Wren laughed and high fived around the table. "Brielle would have never treated me like this."

"That's because Brielle likes you."

"Bring her next time. I thought you would at least be on my side," Terry chuckled.

"Nah, not today, pops," Wren and Nadia giggled at the same time.

wame Franklin

AFTER NADIA STORMED OUT HIS OFFICE, THE SWAY OF her hips was stuck in his mind and it had him up the better part of the night. Today's brunch came as a very pleasant distraction from Nadia's luring presence, even when she wasn't anywhere near him. Working so close to her was making his feelings rise more by the day. It was affecting how he handled women. He found himself not checking for anyone.

Arriving at his father's house, he squinted his eyes, spotting Wren and Nadia's cars parked in the driveway. "What the hell are they doing here?"

Kwame groaned at the thought of having to look at Nadia another day, control himself and possibly apologize for aggravating her the day before. Exiting his car, he walked into the house and followed the sound of laughter coming from the kitchen. Stepping into the kitchen, he spotted Nadia, Wren and Farrah enjoying breakfast alongside Terry.

"What are y'all doing here? Sundays are my day." Wren looked over her shoulder at her brother and rolled her eyes. "Don't roll your eyes at me."

"Kwame, you sound like a damn child," Wren huffed, returning to eating her food. Nadia hadn't even remotely flinched at his presence. "Grab a waffle and hush."

"Good morning, son," Terry stood from the table and hugged him. "Happy there's another man here. Y'all can stop ganging up on me."

Farrah laughed as Wren snorted with laughter. "The fact you think Kwame can save you from anything is hilarious to me."

Her laughter was so contagious, Nadia cracked a small smile. "Nadia, what are you laughing at?"

Immediately, her smile dropped, and her eyes shot daggers in his direction. "Oh, if looks could kill," Terry smirked and bounced his eyes between the two.

"Nah, I'm good," Nadia conceded and went back to finishing up her breakfast.

Kwame stepped back from his father to examine Nadia's once relaxed state. She wore a pair of leggings and her UCLA alumni t-shirt, her messy hair and her makeup-free face made the right side of his mouth form a smirk. He figured if he mustered up enough empathy, he could apologize for being an asshole. After all, his apologies normally smoothed over their issues for a short amount of time.

Lowering himself into the empty seat by Nadia, he folded his arms on the table and looked at her. "My bad for yesterday. I didn't mean to upset you."

All eyes were on the two of them while Nadia scoffed and chuckled. "That hurt you, didn't it?"

"Nah, I mean it."

"No, you don't. Your apology is only for you. To make you feel like it's over and done with. You are an asshole. I can't be mad at who you are, but I don't have to fuck with you. I don't fuck with you. Now, if you all would excuse me, some of us have work to do."

Ejecting herself from the table, she picked up her empty plate, placed it in the dishwasher and headed down the hall to get her gym bag. Nadia said her goodbyes to everyone but Kwame as she exited the house. The second the front door closed; Wren shot a look across the table. "Why?"

"I'll tell you why," Terry spoke up with a smirk etched into his cheeks. "That girl is begging you to tame her ass and you just keep missing the target."

"Would you stop?" Farrah shook her head and stood to her feet. "Every woman who is mean to you doesn't necessarily want to be tamed, as you so eloquently put it. She may just not like you."

"Kwame thinks that every woman who gives him an inkling of an attitude needs to be tamed, like they're a damn horse. Once his mission is accomplished, he drops them like a bad habit. I thought I had issues, but I just realized you have a fear of commitment," Wren watched Kwame's body language go from arrogant to uncomfortable. "Ah! You're uncomfortable, aren't you? Everyone isn't going to be a notch in your belt, brother. Leave my best friend alone before she ends up knocking your teeth out your mouth."

Kwame cleared his throat and took a plate from the middle of the table and helped himself to breakfast. "Why do we always have to resort to violence?"

"Because that seems to be the only thing you understand."

"How was your date, li'l bit?" Kwame swiftly tried to change the subject to get the heat off of him.

"You're a day late. Next."

"I swear, I can't catch a break when I come over here with you."

Terry snapped his fingers and pointed at Farrah and Wren. "You see what I go through. Every Sunday, I get ganged up on because of these two and any guests that come with your sister. Son, all my life I had to fight."

"Terry, quit being dramatic," Farrah smacked her lips and tugged at his ear. "Wren, come look at these shoes I just got."

Farrah picked up on Kwame's discomfort and decided it was best to leave the men alone to have a conversation without any additional commentary. Once Farrah and Wren were gone, Terry poured another cup of coffee and looked over at his son.

"Speak up, son."

Kwame sat back in his seat and didn't make eye contact with his father. He just inhaled and exhaled before leaning forward on his elbows. "You look exhausted."

"I am," Kwame admitted. "This player shit is getting old and exhausting."

Terry hummed before nodding his head. It took his son less time to come to this conclusion than it took him. Pride filled his eyes as he looked at his son. "Most of us don't realize that until it's too late and we're old, just looking for someone to die with. What's keeping you from settling down, though?"

"It's LA," Kwame chuckled. "I don't even know where to start. Plus, I'm not remotely ready to settle down. I'm just tired is all. I've been cooling it."

"I bet you have."

"What does that mean?" he asked, pinning his brows together.

Terry chuckled. "You're smart. Don't play stupid."

"What you talking about? Nadia? I just be bothering her because she's an easy ass target. That's a bag of issues I don't have the time nor the patience to unpack."

"And you don't?" Terry twisted his face. "You can't heal what you don't reveal. You don't need to be laying down with everyone all the time either to feel like a man. That's on me for not showing you that. Unpack your shit and work on your heart before you start seeking someone else's."

Kwame let his father's words sink in and marinate on his heart. There wasn't any need to respond to him. They both knew this journey and Terry wasn't going to let his son travel alone. Terry had failed his children before, and he vowed to never do it again. Kwame had become a man without him, but Terry would never miss the opportunity to guide his son into another level of being a man.

Most men waited until they were ready to fix themselves and break hearts in the process of discovering who they were. It was believed that everyone had time to settle down, that life would wait on them. But anyone from the streets of LA would let you know you didn't have time. It was all an illusion to a narrative that needed to be forgotten. It was a time, in Terry's life, that the Franklin men stepped up to the plate and did right by their women and set the tone for the next generation to follow them.

"You need to understand that, until you heal you, you will never be enough for a real woman and she will never be enough for you. You will look for things in her that you should've possessed the entire time. Remember that."

"You're always dropping gems like you're the Gandhi of

Baldwin Hills." Kwame laughed at his statement and started eating.

"I am the Gandhi of the hood, what are you talking about? You wouldn't know that because your momma moved you out," Terry snickered, bringing his mug to his lips.

"I think it would be dope to go back. Roman had to go into Compton and no one knew him, which is crazy to me because his pops was big time."

"Son, I'm only going to say this once. When you make it out of where I made it out of and you built something for yourself, don't go back looking for validation."

oman Daniels

DAYS HAD GONE BY AND THE ONLY THING ON HIS MIND was Wren. She'd gone from being a thought to becoming a full-blown itch that he needed to scratch. Even if she wasn't going to acknowledge his presence, he just needed to be close enough to her to inhale her scent. She was for sure a drug that he was addicted to. Something so potent and he let it slip right through his fingers. After his conversation with Kamaiyah, he released that at the least he needed to apologize for how he handled the matter of her heart without care. Or with no regard of how she would feel by his selfish need not to be the bad guy in the end.

He was.

He loved her more than she could know. His inability to communicate that properly landed them in the situation they were in today.

"Why are you in my house?" Brielle asked, holding Daniel on her hip.

Ever since Keera decided that she needed to go and find herself, Brielle had to dive head first into mothering a child that she didn't birth. Roman had to take his hat off to both Brielle and Julian for mending things the way they did. It was truly a testimony. Roman thought that if Julian could get his wife back, after everything he put her through, he could definitely get Wren back. With a little push in the right direction, of course.

That was the reason he was sitting in their living room, holding their daughter, trying to soften Brielle up enough to tell him where Wren was.

Roman offered her a lopsided grin and Brielle rolled her eyes and waved him off. "What do you want, Roman?"

"Why do I have to want something to come see about you? We're family."

"Boy, all three of y'all must've gone to the same school of lyin' and failed. What's this about?" Brielle continued to push. "Lie to me again and I'm putting your ass out my house."

"You mean," Roman replied dramatically looking at Brielle's very serious face. "Alright, I quit. Where is Wren?"

"Do I look like the human GPS, Roman Daniels?"

"I mean..." Throwing a bottle at him, Brielle narrowed her eyes. "I'm playing! Damn, girl!"

"Why don't you ask Nadia or call Wren?"

Roman flinched as Brielle lowered her hand and smirked, realizing she had nothing else to throw. "Wren has me blocked and you know damn well Nadia isn't going to help me."

"Then, why the hell should I help you? You've had more chances than K. Michelle and you want my help? I am not about to help you so you can fumble her heart again. She's having a hard enough time getting over your bum ass, I am not about to have a hand in putting her through it again."

"Damn that's what you think about me?" Roman wasn't surprised by Brielle's unwillingness to help him get back in good with Wren.

"No, I think less of you. And stop cursing around my damn babies, boy."

"My bad. If you tell me where she is, I'll leave you alone."

"I knew it. I'm only good for watching babies and throwing undeserving niggas assists. This shit is sad."

"Didn't you just tell me to stop cursing?" Roman asked confused, raising his eyebrow.

"You will learn to do as I say not as I do. Wren is at an open house in Calabasas. I'll text you the address. Make it count, okay?" Brielle's posture relaxed slightly as she connected eyes with Roman. "Please. She's never going to admit it, but she needs you. You might've been inconsistent, for whatever reason, but you were her haven. Please, don't mess this up. If you love her, tell her that. If you want her back, fight for her. Don't let her go again."

Roman nodded his head and stood to his feet. Taking Lillian from his arms, Brielle smiled softly. "Thank you."

"The next time you bring your ass over here, it better be with food and wine."

Roman laughed lightly and winked at her before stepping back and shooting out the door. He knew how Wren ran her open houses. It didn't take long for her to convince anyone that they needed to buy anything. She could sell an ice cube to a polar bear and not bat an eye. As he drove to Calabasas, he recited his lines over and over again.

I want you back. I told you I wasn't letting up off you.

Why are you playing you know this where you want to be?

Baby, I am not leaving here without you.

Nothing sounded convincing or offered him any security that she'd actually fold. Their last conversation played over in his mind. She didn't believe that he was going to come around and demand to love her. This was already going to be an uphill climb for him without that added insult to injury, so he needed to come correct or not at all.

He slipped into the open house, once he reached the location Brielle sent him. There were about six people, including Brielle, huddled in the backyard of the house. Roman roamed around the house, admiring the layout. He was willing to play the back until she noticed him. If she was unwilling to talk to him today, he was going to show up at every open house she had until she broke down and talked to him.

Hearing the glass door slide open, Roman looked over his shoulder to see the group break up and a few couples walk out of the house. Wren smiled and offered her farewells to a few people before spotting Roman.

Instantly, her annoyance spiked and her eyes rolled. She pursed her lips and her hip popped out, as she folded her arms across her chest. This was the last person on earth she wanted to see but she couldn't deny that the sight of him made her heart flutter.

It didn't matter what he was here to say to her, she wasn't going to hear any of it. In fact, she started gathering her things as quickly as she could. "Wren."

"If you aren't here to buy this five-million-dollar house then there is absolutely nothing that we need to talk about."

Her statement was final. She threw her bag over her shoulder and glared at him with her hand on her hip.

"I mean, I could. It's dope."

"Then cut me a check and get the hell out of my face."

"Is that how you talk to your potential clients?" Roman teased but Wren was unresponsive to it. She tried as hard as she could to play dead, dumb, deaf and mute to him. Roman would come back in like a wrecking ball and she didn't want to feel its pain of losing him again.

"Only that you're not. A potential pain in my ass? Yes. A client? No. I can't lock up until you leave, so please go."

Before Roman could walk away, Wren had answered a phone call and strolled out the house, waiting for him to leave. What Wren didn't know was that he had nothing but time and opportunity to get back what he wanted. She was going to be his again, for real, she just didn't know that. Wren could fight as much as she wanted, but she would see.

For the time being, Roman backed off and walked to his car. Walking past her, he gave Wren a devilish smirk that made her eye twitch. The seed was planted. She would think about him more than she was already.

Wren Franklin

Her eye twitched uncontrollably, as she watched his car pull off from the curb. Once he was out of sight, she stomped back into the house and slammed the door.

"It's a shame I had to fake a phone call to get his ass away from me," she muttered to herself while she hit Nadia's name in her contacts.

"What's up, Wren?" Nadia greeted, answering the phone after a couple of rings.

"Don't you 'what's up' me." Wren's snappy attitude was at the hand of Roman and, if she could see Nadia roll her eyes heavily through the phone, her attitude would have intensified. "Did you send Roman over here to vex my nerves, girl?"

Nadia sighed heavily through the receiver. "I know I have a habit of sticking my nose where it doesn't belong, but I haven't even heard from him. You haven't expressed to me that you missed him, or that you've really wanted to get that old thing back. With that, I left it alone."

"Mhmm."

"Don't 'mhmm' me. What happened?" Nadia was ready with an empty cup to catch the tea the Wren was about to serve.

"His ass showed up to my open house."

"Wren," Nadia chuckled through the phone. "At the wedding, what did that man tell you?"

"Nothing important," Wren's voice dropped low enough to make Nadia strain her ears to hear what she had to say.

"Lying must run in your family," Nadia sassed, making Wren narrow her eyes and curl her lip. "What did he tell you, Wren?"

"He told me that he will apply pressure until I'm his again," Wren began to whine like a child while chewing on her bottom lip. "I don't want him anywhere near me."

"You're a liar," Nadia said with a laugh. "You better buckle up, buttercup. A man who says that ain't bullshitting with you. And if you wanted him to leave you alone, we wouldn't be on the phone talking about him. Get your man, girl!"

"I really do not like you right now."

"You'll be thanking me when your back is getting blown out and your hair is being pulled and all is right in your world again," Nadia chuckled before Wren hung up on her.

"She gets on my damn nerves. He's not getting me back that easily," Wren mumbled to herself while tapping her phone against her nails. For a moment, she let her mind trail off to Roman and all the memories they shared together. It wasn't a secret that she loved him with everything she had. But she was learning to love herself more and Roman couldn't come back into her life and undo everything she'd done without him.

She broke herself out of her thoughts and tidied up the house for tomorrow's showing. The mission was to sell this house as fast as she could so Roman couldn't pop back up on her again. Just the five minutes that she was in his presence had her mind spinning. She wanted nothing more than to feel his lips on her skin, or to feel his warmth, but would never give in that easily to him.

Once she got home, she kicked her heels off and plopped down on the couch. Pulling her phone out of her pocket, she called Brielle.

"Hey, my baby," Brielle greeted innocently.

"Drop the act! I know it was you," Wren sassed, looking at her nails. "Your intention was pure, but I would have liked a heads up."

"Why? Did you bust it open?"

"No! Who do y'all think I am?"

"Who you've always been," Brielle snickered. "But did you two get your shit worked out? I'm tired of not having everyone together because the four of y'all can't get it right."

"Leave me out of the four of you. What those two got

going on has nothing to do with what is happening between Rome and me."

"Do you miss him?"

"I would be lying if I said no. I'm just not in the business of giving my heart away again, only to be left looking stupid."

"You won't. Stick to your guns and, whatever you feel, lay it on the table. You'll be good, okay."

"Okay, mama." Wren inhaled and let it go. "When are you going to make Julian watch the babies and come hang out with Nadia and me?"

"Soon. I need a break before I burn this house down and fake like I didn't," Brielle grunted. "Let's shoot for this weekend."

"Alright, I'll see you soon."

Hanging up, Wren looked at her phone and found herself scrolling through photos of her and Roman. A lone tear dropped from her eye and fell on her lap. Quickly wiping her face, she locked her phone and toyed with the idea of entertaining him again. She was uncertain about their future because she was still deeply rooted in their past.

ren Franklin

THREE DAYS HAD PASSED BY AND ROMAN MANAGED TO pop up every single day. She only grew more annoyed with his persistence, until she couldn't take it anymore. Wren knew that he wasn't going to go anywhere until she acknowledged him. So, she waited until the last person was out of the house. Locking the door behind the last couple, she walked into the open living room of the house where Roman was propped against the wall.

"What do you want?"

Roman let his lips curl upward before pushing himself off the wall. "You already know what I want... I've told you."

Laughter took over Wren's being as she shook her head in amusement. "You are just like every other nigga who realizes what they want when it's too late to do anything about it. You might want me, but I'm good."

Roman didn't believe her by a long shot. She was far too calm to convince him that she was good without him. She hid the hurt he caused far away from him, but Roman saw it dancing her eyes.

"You're lying."

"Roman, seriously. Leave me the hell alone."

Roman shrugged his shoulders and looked away. He wasn't leaving without her expressing her true emotions. "Nah, I'm not."

"What is it going to take to get you to go the fuck away? Hm?" her pressure was rising. "What you want me to say, Rome? You broke my fucking heart and you think you can stalk in the shadows and taunt me to lure me back in to you. I don't want to be with you. I don't want to look at you, smell you, feel you, NOTHING! You lost that shit when you couldn't keep it a hundred with me."

Roman closed the space between them and tried to grab a hold of her but she yanked away from him with tears in her almond eyes. "Don't touch me! You don't get to walk out my life and walk back in when you see that the grass ain't greener on the other side."

She forcefully pushed him away, making him stumble back until he caught himself on the back of the couch. "I was so fucking good to you, Roman. I gave you every single piece of me. Pieces that I didn't have to give to you, I took out a loan on them and gave them to you. You dropped me and picked me up, like you do all of your bad habits. I deserve more than your half-ass sorrys, your stolen time, your pleasant lies. I deserve so much more. And I only stayed around for so long because all the love I should have given myself went to you. And you never once gave it back to me. That's not love, Roman, that's abuse."

She growled lowly, wiping her face. Roman clenched

his jaw tightly, examining her. "You have some power over me and it won't let me let you go. I'm a hostage to it. And as much as I hate you, I love you the same. I am so tired of loving and never being loved back. I'm so tired of giving myself to everyone and you don't even have to decency to step up to the plate. I go for men who are like my father. Selfish, spineless, unbothered irresponsible men who wait until they are old and gray and ready to settle down to repent for their sins. I wanted a father in you. I wanted home in you. I wanted peace in you. All you gave me was pain. For that, I hate you. So bad that it hurts."

Roman sucked in a deep breath as Wren gathered her emotions off the table and sighed. "I can't take back anything I've done to you. I can't erase the pain I caused to your beautiful heart. I have always loved you, I just never knew how to express that. I wasn't raised to show emotion. I didn't have any man in my life who had a woman who could show me the way. I can tell you everything I didn't have. That doesn't take away from ruining the best thing that I have ever had. That was you. You may not believe me, but it has broken me to know how bad I broke you. I don't want to pick up where we left off. Instead, I want to start again."

His eyes were locked on hers. Wren was held under his spell and he was enchanting. "Give me two months for one final claim to your heart. If I fail, I fail and I will let you go. I need just two months."

Wren's guard was back up as she crossed her arms. She studied him in detest, but toyed with the idea of one more shot with him. "If you tell me no, right now, I will leave. But I know you don't want that. I can see it."

"Don't," she warned, chewing on her bottom lip. "Don't make a fool of me again. You get one month, four weeks, to change my mind."

"That's all I need. Trust me, you won't regret it."

"I don't believe it, but we will see. You can see yourself out."

She waited an hour and a half after Roman left to leave. She wanted to be in a better state than her current emotional one. Once she left, she headed straight to Brielle's house. Wren had texted 911 to both Brielle and Nadia and they quickly replied with plans to meet. Arriving at Brielle's home, she knocked on the door twice before Julian pulled it open.

"Hey, li'l bit," he smiled, stepping back to let her in. Wren's petite figure gave way for the nickname Kwame has called her since the beginning of time. "The girls are in the dining room."

"Where are you going?" Wren looked at the keys in his hand and his fresh outfit. Julian, Kwame and Roman were definitely friends because they were always as fresh as they came. Julian wore a fresh, white polo t-shirt and a pair of distressed jeans with Jordans on his feet. "You look like a thot looking for trouble."

"To see what you got Roman crying about now," Julian chuckled and looked at her. "Why are you playing with my boy's heart like this?"

Wren raised her brow and huffed. She found it a bit funny that Julian, of all people, questioned her motives with Roman's heart. Especially because no one he surrounded himself with knew how to handle a heart. Not even him. After surveying his serious expression, Wren opened her mouth to reply to him. "He played with mine. Why not return the same sentiment?"

Julian crossed his arms against his chest and closed the door after Wren walked in. "Please let me and Brielle be an example of what happens when you play with love. If you really love him, lay everything on the table and figure it out."

"Alright, Julian," Wren replied, only to get him off of her back.

"Alright, Wren," he sassed in return before grabbing his keys. "Baby, I'm out!"

"Love you! See you later," Brielle shouted down the hall.

"Love you more."

After Julian's exit, Wren joined the girls in the dining room and helped herself to a plate of food and a glass of wine. "Why are y'all looking at me like that?"

"I don't know, you're the one texting us 911," Nadia spoke up, sipping her wine. "I rushed over here. What's going on?"

"Roman," she answered simply, pouring herself a glass. "After a week of him popping up to my open houses, I finally talked to him."

"And what does he want?" Brielle asked. "Get us to the good part."

"After crying and screaming, I agreed to give him a month of my time. He wants to start over, and I would be fronting if I said I didn't want to see what he was on, this time around," Wren pulled her lip between her teeth and looked wearily at her best friends.

Nadia placed her glass back on the table and hummed. "Are you asking us for approval? I hope not. This is your life and your decision and you have to be okay with that. I just don't know what he can show you that he hasn't already."

"So, I shouldn't?" Wren twisted her face in confusion.

"No. Wren, you need to make a decision that you can live with. Weigh your options. You could be introduced to another side of him that is beautiful, or you could be exposed to the same shit. It's your choice. But I have to say, to love someone is to risk the loss of them. But would you rather love and lose it or never love at all?"

"Being a mother has made you poetic as shit and it's beautiful," Nadia began to fake cry. "That was beautiful."

Wren chewed on her lip and sat back in the chair. "One last shot for everything we got."

"Get in the ring and finish the fight strong. Whoever alluded to the fact that love was easy should be shot. It's not easy and it's not always beautiful but it is *so* worth it," Brielle placed her hand on top of Wren's. "I'll be here with you, every step of the way."

"So will I. Treat this as though he never hurt you and take your time getting to know him. Okay?"

Wren smiled at her friends and nodded her head. Her friends were always in her corner, pushing her to follow her heart. It's been a ride but, she knew, as long as she had them in her corner coaching her while she fought for the love that she deserved, she would be okay.

"Okay." Her response was delayed. Both Brielle and Nadia knew that it didn't matter what they said to her, she would find her way back to Roman, one way or another. As long as her heart was protected, that was the only thing that concerned them. The Libra in Wren needed constant love and affection.

"Good, I got to say your 911 text came at the best time," Nadia smirked.

"You were fighting with Kwame again?" Brielle groaned as Nadia twisted her face. "You two really just don't need to be in the same space."

"Girl, no. I was about to ruin the contractor's life at the

restaurant, if he kept flirting with me." Brielle rolled her eyes and started to laugh at Nadia. "He's not ready for me."

"You are such a man," Wren giggled, tucking her hair behind her ears. "Such a man."

Nadia smiled wide, proud of her inability to get caught up and attached to anyone. "I am. And I am damn good at it."

"Until you meet your match and he breaks you down like some kush." Brielle shrugged her shoulders and refreshed her glass.

"Won't ever happen. Don't wish that death upon me." Nadia's smile dropped and her expression was taken over by seriousness.

"Watch," Wren smirked softly waving her finger in Nadia's direction. "She's going to be head over heels the minute someone finds her and puts the mack down."

"You can't put mack down on a mack," Nadia smacked her lips before changing the subject. "Have y'all heard from Keera?"

"Julian hasn't heard a word from her. We don't even know where she is," Brielle seemed to be completely unbothered by her absence. No one could blame her either. Keera being out the picture had only brought more peace and security to Brielle. "She can either be a mother or not. The choice is hers and has always been. But I will not make that sweet baby suffer because of her inability to do what she's supposed to do. If she pops back up, I'll be shocked my damn self. My expectations of her aren't high at all."

"Well," Nadia shrugged, opening another bottle of wine. "Hopefully the bitch has realized that she's better off away."

"Don't talk her up," Wren groaned.

"If she pops up, I got the biggest of ass whoppings waiting on her."

"You're so Oakland." Brielle rolled her eyes, not wanting to think about the woman who managed to wedge herself between her and her husband. "You have no chill and no desire to find any."

"All day, everyday baby," Nadia smirked. "All day."

ulian Harris

JULIAN COULDN'T HELP BUT FEEL A SENSE OF RELIEF, now that everything was back on track with his marriage and his life overall. Since being transferred to another hospital, he was promoted to the director of the emergency department. What was designed to break him, his marriage and his wife turned out to be the greatest blessing. He had more time to be at home with his family and be a part of the moments that mattered.

He wanted his boys to experience the same warm, overwhelming feeling of walking into the house after a long day and be greeted by people who loved you. Loved your good, bad and the ugly parts that you hid away from everyone. That was a life worth living. At some point, the games had to come to a stop, and they had to man up.

They sat around the table and shared their normal

banter. "You know, I never understood the reason you insisted on wearing black," Roman chuckled, looking at Kwame who was dressed in a black Lacoste polo tucked into a pair of black slacks. Out of the entire group, Kwame didn't lack in style.

"You need to be focused on Wren dropping the dime to the old man about you and not what I chose to wear today," Kwame pointed across the table before taking a drink from his glass.

Roman's eyes grew wide as Julian chuckled. "I told your simple ass to get a plan before you went all crazy trying to get her back. Disorganized and triflin', I swear."

"Cheaters anonymous, mind your business," Roman grunted.

"I owned my shit. Been there and I'm back. You're the one trying to get back with no plan."

Kwame winced slightly and waved his finger over at Julian. "I got to admit that the cheating bandit is right on this one. No plan is going to cause you to be assed out."

"Pause."

"Anyway," Roman huffed. "I have a plan. Thank you."

"And..." Kwame leaned back in his seat before shifting his eyes over to Julian. "I can't wait to hear this half-baked idea."

"Me neither. You know he lacks imagination." Julian and Kwame dapped hands and laughed while Roman's grimace took over his face. "We got to chill. The little baby is about to cry."

Kwame's wide smile faded into a smirk as he looked at Roman. "Alright, tell us the plan."

"After hard negotiation she gave me a month a month to prove that I am for real."

Kwame and Julian both raised their eyebrows and

looked at Roman without saying anything. They had given him the time he needed to fully explain himself and they were expecting a lot more. "That's it? You plan on getting her back by being in her face for a month?"

Julian's confusion eased into a hearty laugh and Kwame joined in. "I will never tell you two shit else. I'm going to get her back, just watch."

"We're going to be watching. I got the beer," Kwame assured, leaning up on his elbows as the waitress strutted over. She'd been trying to get Kwame's attention since they sat down but Kwame hadn't even looked twice in her direction.

"Y'all got to have more faith in me," Roman groaned, running his hand over his waves as the waitress stopped at the table to put the checks down. "I got it."

She smiled wearily before walking away. Roman looked down at the checks and smiled at Kwame. "You didn't say two words to her and you still got her number."

"Who said pimping was dead?" Kwame smirked, resting against the table.

"My dawg," Julian chuckled.

"Bow wow," Kwame replied as Julian pulled out his wallet and began flipping through his cards. "He's about to pull that shit on us."

Julian reached for his wallet and shook his head. "Remember, he did this the day before graduation."

"I always come prepared now, because of that," Kwame added.

Roman pulled out a card and waved them off. "I said I got. I got it. What I don't have is my debit card." He sat back and closed his eyes and inhaled deeply before releasing it. "I'm about to bash her head through a wall."

Once he was calm enough to settle his breathing, he

pulled up the banking app on his phone and logged in to see where the card was last used. "I told that sneaky ass girl to go in my wallet for a few bucks and she took my damn card. And she's back in Compton."

"How you know that?" Julian raised his brow.

"She swiped it at a store. I'm going down there. I'll get up with y'all later."

"Nah, we're coming, too," Kwame spoke up while standing from his seat. "If you're riding, so are we."

oman Daniels

MORE THAN ANYTHING, HE WAS WORRIED. SINCE Kamaiyah had been with him, they set up a system. Whatever she needed, whatever she wanted, he would get it without hesitation, but she had to be real with him and tell him what was going on. This just set their relationship back. Roman wanted to trust that she wouldn't pull any shit, but he clearly saw that she was taking his kindness for weakness.

"I'm going to fuck her ass up," Roman grumbled to himself, gripping the steering wheel. "I talked to her about this shit."

"Chill, Ro. She's a teenage girl," Kwame spoke from the back seat, trying to settle Roman. There wasn't any talking to him. "They think they know it all."

"Nah." Roman objected to Kwame's words and sped

down the street. Everyone was holding on to the handles while Roman whipped the car through traffic.

Julian and Kwame didn't dare say anything until Roman slowed down and started scanning the area for Kamaiyah. He'd called her over a dozen times and she hadn't answered once. His heart was in his stomach while his mind raced, trying to figure out where she was and who she was with. Initially, he thought that she'd come back to see a few old friends until she disabled her location. He realized quickly that Kamaiyah was up to something and he was going to get to the bottom of it.

He drove around for another fifteen minutes before spotting her on a bus bench. "There she goes."

Without warning, he slammed on the brakes, threw the car in park, in the middle of traffic and got out. After a light jog, he stopped at her feet and looked down at her. Kamaiyah avoided making eye contact with him but Roman wasn't having any more of her nonsense. "Look at me."

His growl was as low as her eyes were. They were red and puffy. Everything in him was screaming to snatch her up but, instead, he nodded his head towards the car. "Get in."

Kamaiyah did as she was told and climbed into the back seat next to Kwame and looked out the window.

Just as fast as Roman got to her, he got home just as quickly. The minute his foot crossed the threshold of the door, his temper boiled over. He managed to hold his tongue the entire ride but couldn't do it any longer.

"Are you out of your rabid ass mind?" he nudged her further into the condo while Julian and Kwame stood by the door, watching the interaction between the two of them. "You had my heart in my damn ass, looking for you!"

"Well, I'm fine, Ro. Chill out," Kamaiyah huffed, trying

to walk away from him. Roman was faster than her. Grabbing her by the arm, tight enough to pull her back, he closed the space between them. "Quit!"

"No! What the fuck were you thinking? Take my card and run off like I wasn't going to find you. Why the hell were you even down there? I thought we talked about this, Kamaiyah!" Roman's voice was bouncing off the walls and if he didn't get a grip sooner than later, Kamaiyah was going to shut down.

"You care, now! Where have you been, Roman? M.I.A. You weren't checking for me or mom. So, cut it out with the fake concern. I don't need it. I was good before you tried to fly in with your cape!" Kamaiyah's voice was just as loud as Roman's. She heaved in and out, staring him down like she was fearless. The tears cradled in her eyes told everyone watching the opposite.

Julian stepped in to push Roman away from Kamaiyah. "Ro, chill! This is not how you're going to get answers out of her and she's not going to respond to anything else. Cool out."

Roman placed his hands on the top of his head and stepped back, instantly feeling horrible for popping off on her like that. He wanted to show her a better man and he felt like he was failing miserably. "Maiyah, you good?"

Julian examined her anxious demeanor. Before Kamaiyah could reply, she threw up all over Julian. Releasing a low groan, Julian stood still, looking at the vomit drip down his body. "I am so sorry," Kamaiyah apologized before barreling down the hall to the bathroom.

"Oh, God," Kwame winced not daring to step closer to them. "I'm going to be sick."

Roman stood behind Julian with his mouth open. "Don't move. I got clothes."

"What?" Kwame asked, twisting his face up. "He can't fit none of your shit, tiny Tim."

"Just go get my gym bag out the trunk of my car," Julian directed, slowly inching into Roman's room to take his soiled clothes off. "Ro, you need to cool your ass down and get in there and talk to her."

Leaving Julian to change, Roman walked down the hall and tapped his knuckles on her door. "Go away!"

"Open the door, Maiyah," Roman spoke into the door waiting for her to open it. A few moments passed before he heard the knob twist and Kamaiyah slowly opened the door before she turned to walk away from him. He stepped in and closed the door behind him, leaning his back on it and looked at her. "What's going on with you? I thought we had an understanding?"

Kamaiyah nervously chewed on her bottom lip and avoided looking at his face. She sat down on the edge of her bed, on top of her hands. "I called Franco to tell him that I'm pregnant and he told me to get rid of it."

The air left Roman's body. His posture stiffened as Kamaiyah dropped her head and took a few deep breaths. "He said that if I didn't do it, he was going to do it. So, I took your card and headed down there to get rid of it. But they wouldn't let me because I'm not eighteen. I guess it's a good thing because I really didn't want to get rid of it."

Kamaiyah cried softly and Roman started breathing again. "Hey, hey. Stop that," Roman sat down by her and pulled her into his arms. "It's okay."

"No, it isn't, Ro. I fuck everything up," she sobbed into his chest. Swallowing his emotions, he kissed the top of her head.

"Stop that. Wipe your face. Ain't no need to cry now.

The deed is done, your decision is made. Don't you worry about that nigga. You hear me?"

Kamaiyah nodded her head and wrapped her arms around Roman. "I'm so sorry, I didn't know what else to do."

"Don't you ever think that you have to make a decision on your own. As long as I'm here, you will always be good. You hear me?"

"I hear you."

"Good. Go get cleaned up."

He had a name. He was going to run down on Franco, one way or another.

 ren Franklin

STEPPING OUT OF THE SHOWER TO GRAB HER PHONE, she groaned, seeing the name flash on her screen. Swiping the button on the screen, Wren sighed heavily before pressing it against her ear. "I thought you were going to wait on my answer."

Roman ignored her and started talking. "I know this isn't your job, but I need you to do me a solid. Can you get over here as soon as you can?"

The urgency in his voice shot adrenaline through her body. "I'm on my way."

Where their relationship, or lack thereof, was at the moment didn't matter. He needed her and she was going to show up. Quickly getting dressed, she grabbed her phone and sent a text to Nadia and Brielle, telling them to meet her at Roman's house.

She flew across town to get to his condo. By the time she

parked the car, Nadia and Brielle were standing by the elevator in leggings, t-shirts and sneakers. No one could ever say that they didn't ride for each other. No matter what they were going through, all it took was one phone call and they were ready to ride.

"Listen," Nadia started as Wren got closure to her. "I didn't know if I had to beat his ass, so I brought my Vaseline."

Brielle flailed her arms up in the air and shook her head before hitting the button for the elevator. "I was just about to ask you what was in that bag."

"I brought my gun, too."

"Why do you have a gun?" Brielle asked, widening her eyes.

"Because I didn't know what the hell we were about to walk into." Nadia stepped onto the elevator behind Wren and Brielle. "I got to cover all bases. If we are slicing and dicing people, then I need to be prepared. Since you're judging me, I'm not telling you that I have shower caps, gloves and trash bags in here,too."

Wren chuckled, followed by a sigh. "I don't know what's going on, but he sounded like he needed help."

Stepping off the elevator, Wren pulled out her key to let them in, only to see Kwame, Julian and Roman standing in the kitchen. Wren was confused. "Is everything okay?"

Brielle furrowed her eyebrows and looked at Julian's outfit. "That is not what you left the house in."

"Kamaiyah had an accident," Julian shared.

"Damn! It takes all of y'all to watch one girl?" Kwame asked, looking over them.

Nadia sucked her teeth and dropped her bag. "I come over here ready for war only to find out I'm babysitting?

Dang it, I was ready to beat somebody's ass." Nadia dropped into a chair and crossed her legs.

"Fill me in," Wren spoke up, looking at Roman's hiked shoulders and his pensive expression.

"Maiyah got wrapped in some nigga and I'm going to go see him. I just need y'all to keep your eyes on her until I can get back," Roman didn't look at her. He knew that Wren had the power to calm him down and he wanted to remain in this headspace until he was done doing what he had to.

Wren nodded her head. "Is she okay?"

"Okay and pregnant," Julian shared, leaning forward on the countertop.

"She's lying down. Watch your wallets around her. She's fast," Kwame shared before Julian and Roman shot him a look. "What? I'm not lying. I've been checking my pockets every time she walks past me."

"I swear," Julian groaned, placing his hand on his forehead. "Something is wrong with you."

"Something is wrong with you to think that she won't hustle you out a few bucks. She's slick. I got to give her that," Kwame shrugged his shoulders.

Roman kissed his teeth before looking at Wren. "Thanks. I owe you one."

"Yeah, you do," Nadia spoke up. "All of us. I was about to ruin someone's life and I dropped everything, thinking I was going to put you into trash bags."

Roman's face twisted as he tilted his head to the side looking at Nadia as if she had fully lost her mind. Wren quickly spoke up turning the attention from Nadia to the task at hand, "Ignore her. We got her. Be safe, okay?"

Roman smiled down at her and caressed her cheek with his thumb. "Always."

Wren smirked and caught her breath before she lost it.

Things like this were reasons that she loved him the way she did. He was a protector in every sense of the word. She could see the change in him because she was still. When she was raging in her emotions, she wanted him to be the same man that left her hanging. He wasn't.

"Alright, let's go before I change my mind," Kwame broke up their moment and nudged Roman toward the door.

Once the door closed, Nadia looked at Wren and smirked. "Were you ever going to give him his key back?"

"Why would I do something like that?" Wren asked as Brielle and Nadia rolled their eyes. Wren bit down on her lip slightly and squeezed her eyes shut.

"We should've known. That man has her bent over a barrel," Nadia snickered, high fiving Brielle.

"Where is Roman?" Kamaiyah's voice interrupted the laughter between Brielle and Nadia. "Who are you?"

"I'm Wren. That's Nadia and Brielle. We're friends of Roman," Wren introduced the girls to Kamaiyah, who wasn't as receptive as Wren imagined she would be.

"So, Roman called babysitters to make sure I didn't do what?"

When Nadia turned around and looked at Kamaiyah, her heart dropped. Kamaiyah's attitude was screaming for someone to hear her and tell her it was going to be okay. She reminded Nadia a lot of where she was as a seventeen-year-old girl, with the pain and questions. Standing to her feet, she examined Kamaiyah.

"I don't know. You tell us," Nadia intervened as Kamaiyah tried to avoid eye contact with her. "What do you need?"

"To not be treated like a child because he isn't comfortable with me being alone."

Nadia sighed and leaned on the back of the chair she was previously sitting in. "Dial back for a second and thank God you have someone to protect you. Go put some shoes on. We're going to eat."

ROMAN DANIELS

THEY REACHED COMPTON IN RECORD TIME. ROMAN had already summoned the help of Ronnie to locate Franco, and Kwame and Julian were both ready for whatever would happen next. Roman knew that whatever was to happen, his boys were going to ride with him until the wheels fell off. They were a group of boys from the hood that made it out and held each other in high regard. It was true, the friends you met in college would be lifetime friendships that you could always rely on. Them riding for him as hard as they did proved that.

"Pull up here, to the left." Roman unbuckled his seatbelt and grabbed his gun out the glovebox before Kwame could pull over and park the car.

"How long have we known him, and we never knew that he was carrying a piece?" Julian asked, leaning from the back seat. "Let me find out you got heart, little nigga."

"Shut up, Julian," Roman muttered, cocking the gun back so that the bullet sat ready in the chamber. "Don't say nothing when Ronnie starts talking."

Exiting the car, Roman placed his foot on the sidewalk and looked around before stepping to Ronnie. "That's his spot?"

"Yeah. His momma is in there. Tell us what you want us

to do, Ro," Ronnie and Roman both looked at the modest home and inhaled the warm night air.

Shrugging his shoulders, Roman took a step back and shook his head. "Bring him out here. I'm not with shooting up a nigga's house and his moms is in there."

Ronnie nodded and stepped away from Roman, starting his pursuit up the walkway to the front door of Franco's house. Roman removed his gloves from his pocket and secured them over his hands. Julian and Kwame were now posted up on Roman's car, intently watching him and Ronnie. Kwame removed his gun out the waist of his sweats and held it, ready for anything.

It seemed like an eternity before Ronnie coaxed Franco out the house. Unknowingly, Franco blindly followed behind Ronnie to the sidewalk. "What's going on?"

"This is Ro, Senior's son," Ronnie introduced him to Roman, who was contemplating how bad he wanted him to pay for disturbing his sister's peace.

Franco nodded his head and looked over at Julian and Kwame before focusing back on Roman. Turning his face back to Roman, he was greeted by the butt of Roman's gun. Slightly stumbling backward, Franco caught himself on the gate and grunted in pain. Roman didn't let up at all. Something took over him. He reverted back to his street ways, in a split-second, thinking about how Franco had messed Kamaiyah's head up. He didn't want to kill Franco, but he wanted him to remember to never cross any member of his family or his set.

Standing up, Roman took the red flag out his pocket and wiped the blood from his face. Franco was sprawled across the sidewalk, like roadkill. Stooping down to his level, Roman looked at him in disgust. "You would be wise not to fuck with no extension of me. My sister. My set. My hood."

Standing upright, Roman handed Ronnie the soiled red bandana and looked him in the eyes. "Just in case anyone around here needed a reminder of who I am and who I come from. Thanks."

Ronnie nodded his head with pride. He thought Roman had lost what made everyone whisper that he was Senior's son. "Stay up, youngblood."

"Always. Thank you."

With that, the two shook hands and parted ways. If Shelia wanted to stay here, that was on her, she would remain protected. As far as Kamaiyah was concerned, she would never return and neither would he. Compton raised him, showed him everything he had the power to turn himself into and showed him everything that he didn't want to be, in the same breath. He didn't want to end up like his parents, dead in a grave and dead in a cage, being held hostage by the mentality of the hood. This chapter of his life was closed, he was thankful for everything the streets taught him but now was the time for him to morph into a man that was better than the OGs, a man better than his father. Time wasn't on his side and he needed to be a better man for himself, for Kamaiyah and for Wren. Everything else was irrelevant to what his heart desired. Irrelevant to the path he was traveling down for a better life.

Climbing back in the car, he removed his gloves and returned them and the gun to the glove box. The ride back to the condo was silent. Kwame's respect for Roman grew, at that moment. Julian smirked to himself to see the growth in Roman. This point propelled them forward, no looking back on yesterday when tomorrow was in view.

Entering his condo, Roman looked around and found a note from Wren on the kitchen counter.

We went out to dinner. Kamaiyah is spending the night with us. Everything is okay... get some rest. Xoxo

A smile crossed his face as he removed his blood-stained hoodie. Throwing it in the trash, he headed to his bedroom. After a hot shower, he stood on the balcony of his room and watched the city life underneath his feet.

"Pops, I'm stepping out of your shadow. Stepping away from what you left behind but holding on to what you taught me. I got Kamaiyah and mom... if she lets me. Just know, your little man ain't so little no more. Anything that tries to stop my growth or going after what I want, what I deserve, won't stand a chance. Thank you for teaching me everything I thought I needed to know. You can rest easy... I got it from here."

wame Franklin

AFTER LAST NIGHT, KWAME COULDN'T HELP BUT relinquish his concerns. Had the shoe been on Kwame's foot, he would've done the same thing for Wren. He'd done a good job of staying out of their mix, but Kwame decided to completely step off. If Wren needed him to pull up, he would. But, as of now, their relationship was on their terms and in their hands.

"The dark skin Casanova," Wren giggled, poking Kwame on both sides of his body, causing him to jump. "Still refuse to giggle in public?"

"You are not about to mess up my pull in these streets," he flashed his million-dollar smile and pulled her seat out for her to sit down. It was second nature for him to stand by the table and wait on her to show up so he could pull her chair out. This was a habit he carried over into his dating life. The women loved it. Hell, they loved him, until the morning after.

Wren smirked at his comment, settling into her seat. "I thought you were retiring from your pimping?"

Kwame returned the gesture and sat down in his seat. "Slowing down doesn't mean that I need my reputation to be smutted in these streets, li'l bit. What you got going on?"

"Nothing but work and you know how that goes," picking up her menu, she leaned back in her seat and began looking for something to tantalize her palette with. "How did last night turn out? I haven't heard from Roman since he picked up his sister this morning."

Simpering slightly, Kwame opened his menu and relaxed a bit. "Last night was real."

"Are you going to elaborate?"

"I'm not."

Wren clicked her tongue against her lips and rolled her eyes. "Hmm."

"What I will say is, I'm proud of him. Roman has really kept true to his word," Kwame shared.

"The thing that bothers me is where was this stand-up guy when I was around?"

Placing his menu down, he looked at his baby sister and exhaled before answering her question. "I can only speak for me. For me, my failure to move forward to be the man I'm supposed to be comes from a place of fear. A place that, knowing if I fail, I'm going to waste her time and mine. In the end, someone is going to lose. Shit, both of us might lose. As a man, you don't want to be held accountable for your trail of broken hearts. But as a man, you have to be. Feel me? We sometimes can be a slow walk in the park. We know where we're going, but it takes a little longer to get there. But when we arrive, we will relish in that. Everyone has to take their path to come into themselves."

"Now that you put it like that, I guess I need to let go of what happened and focus on the now."

"You love him. I know you do. I know that he loves you. That's some beautiful shit. He's stepping up and coming to claim what's his, you need to be willing to get everything you want. Just make sure I get to make a speech at the wedding, alright?"

Wren smiled wide and rolled her eyes. "Thanks, big bro."

"Anytime. My knowledge is going to cost you lunch," picking his menu back up, he looked over it, trying to spot something that was going to settle his stomach.

Wren looked at him and leaned up on her elbows. "I need you to do me a favor."

"I'm out of favors, Wren."

"Come on! Don't be like that," she whined. "Just a little itty-bitty favor."

Kwame looked over his menu at her. "What?"

"Nadia."

He groaned at the name. "What about Satan?"

"Can you find it deep down inside of your cold, petty ass heart to be nicer and not rile her up so much?"

"All that woman understands is cold and petty. I have tried and, every time I'm remotely nice to her, she opens her damn mouth." Wren watched as Kwame squirmed in his seat.

"It sounds like you're fighting something deeper than her just working your nerves. Sounds like you like that shit and you don't want to like that shit."

If Kwame could've turned red, he would've. Wren could feel the extra heat coming off of him. "Don't lie to me either. I know you. That is the only woman in history who has ignored your advances. The only woman who can upset you and the only reason you keep her at arm's length is because you don't want your heart broken again."

"Order your food," Kwame responded, relieved that the waiter appeared to take their orders.

Wren smirked, conceding from pressing the issue any further. However, it didn't stop her from planning on how to get the two together. If they were going to push her back into Roman's arms, she was going to push them into each other's.

KWAME SAT ON HIS COUCH, PULLED OUT HIS PHONE AND began to scroll through his contacts for all the women he had saved. Never were they saved by their names, only by what they could do for him. It was shameful and he groaned at how sickening it was to scroll through his phone and see no one that he could invite over to watch a movie with and enjoy their company without wanting to get rid of them in the morning.

Locking his phone, he turned on the TV and laid across the couch. He could feel his phone vibrate against his leg. Without looking at the name on the screen, he answered it, pressing it against his ear. "Hello."

"I thought you wouldn't answer. It's me..."

His heart dropped into his stomach, causing him to jolt up to his feet. "Keisha?"

"Yeah," she spoke like she was holding her breath.

Kwame's expression was just as confused as he was. He couldn't figure out whether to hang up or apologize for how things ended between them. Keisha was the only woman that he cared for enough to open his heart to. Instead of entering into the realms of his heart, she pulled away. Her pull made Kwame do something he never thought he would: beg for a woman to be transparent. As things turned toxic between the two, they laid a path of hurt and pain for each other. For Kwame, it made trusting someone's motive and loyalty even harder for him.

"What... why are you calling?" he questioned, positioning himself in front of the window overlooking the pool in his backyard. "It's been years."

"I know," she released a heavy breath. "I know... I heard you were in L.A. and I just wanted to meet up and catch up, if you're up to it."

He dropped the phone from his ear and grunted to himself. Opening old wounds could either lead to healing or a deeper cut. He would be lying if he said he wasn't remotely interested in what she had to say. Reluctantly, he placed the phone back to his ear. "Yeah, I'm free tonight."

"Let's meet at Nobu. Is that cool?"

"Yeah. I'll be there at like eight."

"See you then." He hung up and pressed his hands against the window and sighed. A small voice told him to run, as far and fast as he could, in the opposite direction. It would be his curiosity that would kill him.

He sat at a table in the corner, waiting on Keisha to arrive. Seeing her float across the dining room, he felt his heart skip a few beats before gathering himself. As she got closer, he stood up and smiled nervously at her. Her chocolate skin danced under the dim lights of the restaurant and her light fragrance took his mind back to when she used to lie in his arms on lazy Sundays. The dress that she wore was begging to be ripped to shreds.

"Kwame," she smirked, standing a few inches away from him. "You're looking better than I remembered."

"I can say the same for you." He tried to keep his distance from her. She would have him eating out the palm of hands in mere seconds, if he got too close. He pulled her seat out so she could sit down before taking his. "So... we're here."

Keisha rubbed her arms nervously before dragging her eyes across the table to his fixated stare. "Yeah. I needed to look at you and tell you I'm sorry. I wasn't ready for your love back then."

"And you're back because you are now?"

She nodded her head and Kwame sat back in his seat. "I'm not ready to fall back into that space with you. It was hell."

"I understand," she released, defeated by his response.

"We're here. Let's just talk and enjoy dinner. Cool?"

Keisha nodded happily at his offer. As the night went on and the drinks continued to be poured, he found himself falling back into her spell. Walking out of the restaurant behind her, he surveyed the area before stopping by her side. "I enjoyed tonight."

Nodding his head, he let a smile turn the corners of his mouth upward. "I did, too. Thanks for inviting me out."

Keisha pulled him into a hug without warning and inhaled his scent off of the knit shirt he wore. Slowly, she looked up to see him looking down at her. On impulse, their lips met. For a few minutes, they were consumed with one another. The kiss told Kwame that she had more in mind than just dinner. Falling back into his old ways, he followed her home without thinking about what tomorrow would bring for his back step.

14

oman Daniels

LOOKING AT HIMSELF, ONE LAST TIME, IN HIS REARVIEW mirror, he picked up the bouquet of flowers off the passenger seat and pushed the car door open. Walking up the stairs to Wren's apartment, he coached himself through the way he wanted the day to go. Their relationship started off fast in the beginning and he needed to make sure that, this time around, he took his time.

"This is round one. Get to twelve without a knockout. It'll be cool," he huffed, reaching her floor. Sauntering to her door, he stopped and inhaled, resetting himself. Knocking on the door, he waited anxiously for her to pull it open. When the knob turned, his heart began to pound out of his chest.

Wren stood in front of him, wearing a pair of white, high-waisted jeans, a white t-shirt and a pair of blush pink, open-toed sandals. Roman bit his lips slightly before they parted into a smile, showing his perfect teeth. "You look great."

"Thanks," she smiled. "Those are for me?"

"Yeah. I heard you liked peonies and roses. I had to drive around all of Los Angeles to get those for you. Not to brag or nothing," he chuckled as she took the bouquet from his hands and inhaled the scent.

Wren kissed her teeth, "You just had to toot your own horn." Disappearing inside the apartment to put the flowers down, she grabbed her purse and closed the door behind her. "Alright, make my day."

"Who said I wasn't going to?" he asked, letting her travel down the stairs before him. "You gotta have some faith in me."

"I got faith, just not in you," Wren sassed, descending the stairs.

Roman smirked and nodded his head as she trailed to the car ahead of him. "I'll show you. You'll have faith in me before the night is over."

"How much are we betting on it?" Wren asked as Roman unlocked the car and opened her door. "Put your money where your mouth is."

"Betting on it means I have a chance to lose. I already lost once, I never lose twice." Wren climbed inside, bit her lip and grunted at his response.

Traveling around the city with the music blasting, Roman was enjoying just having her by his side again. He knew Wren was looking for an expensive display of trying to win her back, but he had something else in mind. Pulling into a parking lot where a taco truck was located, he parked and killed the engine. "Come on, let's eat."

After he opened her door, he grabbed a towel out his

trunk and trailed behind her to the taco truck. "What do you want?"

"You already know what I want," Wren spoke up over her shoulder. "Let's see if you can get it right."

"I don't know why you're testing me like this. Of course, I remember what you want. Watch this." He was confident, as he stepped up to the window to order for them. "I need five chicken tacos with extra limes and salsa verde and six braised beef tacos."

"I get six tacos," she smacked her lips, rolling her eyes.

"And you don't ever get to the sixth taco. Better quit acting up before I give you a reason to roll your eyes," he mumbled, hoping she didn't hear his smart comment. Nudging his shoulder, she stomped away. Roman smiled and paid for the food and walked over to a picnic bench. Laying the towel on the seat, he motioned for her to sit down. "You're spoiled as hell, you know that?"

"You made me this way," she shrugged, taking a seat.

"No, I didn't. That was your daddy and your brother. You were spoiled long before I put my hands on you." Although Terry had been absent most of her life that didn't stop him for spoiling her as an adult. Wren could be fifty years old and Terry would still try to compensate for the time he lost with his daughter.

"I guess. You might be right."

"Does it hurt so bad to say, you're right Roman?"

"Yes. It burns my soul to even think about letting those words escape my lips."

Roman shook his head and smiled. He was happy just to be in her presence and put a smile on her face. This was a new day and a new beginning to the love story he wanted to write with her. After Wren struggled to get her five tacos down and prove that she could eat six, they headed to the beach.

They walked the stretch, getting lost in the waves crashing against the shore while engaging in small talk, here and there, and watching the tide come in and recede. Wren spotted a bench and climbed up the hill to sit down. Roman joined her and looked out at the horizon. "Tell me something..."

Wren pushed her hair out her face and looked over at him, staring into the distance. "What's on your mind?"

"In five years, where do you want to be?"

Wren shrugged her shoulders and leaned back into the bench, crossing her legs and arms. "Owning my own real estate agency, in a relationship... a healthy relationship. Owning my own house. Overall, I just want to be happy. How about you? Where do you see yourself in five years?"

Roman grinned and looked over into her brown face before speaking. "Maybe a few more body shops, owning my own house, enjoying my life with my family... with you."

Wren swallowed hard and looked back at the water. "With me?"

Roman dropped his head back and licked the salt from the ocean breeze from his lips. "With you."

"Why?"

"You sure you want to know why?" he questioned, making her nudge him in the ribs playfully. "Be careful what you ask for."

"Just answer my question and stop being difficult, man," Wren giggled.

"There's a variety of reasons why I want to be with you," he started after a couple of seconds of silence. "Why I want to spend my days with you. The biggest one, I know what it's like to be without you. I lived that life of walking around feeling like I was naked because I didn't have my covering. That's the main reason why I see my future with you in it. The other reason... Shit! You make me look good. You make me feel good. It's not even about sex, but don't get it twisted that was a great bonus. But your heart and how you care and ride for what you believe in and what you love, I want that... nah, I need that."

Wren pulled her lips between her teeth while Roman explained his answer to her. "I'm leveling up and I don't want to go to this next level without you. It's not every day a man meets his soulmate, drunk in a club and takes her down the first time..."

"Shut up! I thought we promised not to bring that up again," Wren whined with a giggle as Roman pulled her into his arms. "I was drunk and out my mind."

"But when you woke up, you remembered it."

"I did," Wren admitted, rolling her eyes.

"But, seriously, all I want is you and everything that comes with it."

Wren rested her head on his shoulder and processed the soul food he gave her to chew on. A rebuttal wasn't needed. She melted into his body and inhaled his scent while they watched the sunset over the horizon. Before the sun could fully disappear over the coast, Roman tilted Wren's head back ever so slightly by the root of her hair. Hovering his lips over hers, he smirked lightly seeing the anticipation flood her eyes. He caressed the tip of his nose against hers before kissing her supple lips. With their tongues engaged, Wren moaned softly, placing her hand on his chest. His heart beat heavily against her hand at the same rhythm hers was pounding.

Roman pulled and smiled down at her. "Let me get you home before I violate your ass on this bench."

After dropping Wren off, Roman grabbed a few burgers from In and Out and headed home. Kamaiyah was wide awake in the living room, flipping through channels. "How was your date?"

Roman couldn't help the happiness plastered across his face. He couldn't hide it if he wanted to. "It was cool."

"From the way you bounced in here, with that goofy ass smile on your face, it was better than cool," Kamaiyah smirked, reaching for the bag of food. "Give me."

"Does the word 'please' exist in your vocabulary?"

"No. I'm starving."

Relinquishing custody of the bag over to her, he sat in the armchair and watched the figures move across the screen. "You gave any thought to how you're going to take care of the baby?"

"It's all I think about. I don't know, honestly. I'm just trying to make it through graduation."

"Well, listen. I'm not going to put you out with a baby, but I *am* going to push you to be a responsible adult. So, you start at the shop the day after graduation. You'll clock in at nine and clock out at five. No shit, no excuses. I'll cover your health insurance and you're responsible for the water bill."

"And how am I going to get from here to work?"

"Your ass is spoiled as hell. Let's see how your grades look before I jump off the cliff and buy a bus pass."

ren Franklin

"I NEED TO KNOW WHY YOU HAVE THAT HUGE SMILE plastered across your face," Nadia spoke up from behind her phone that had been consuming her since she waltzed into Wren's office and threw her feet up on her desk.

Wren didn't even mind looking at the soles of her shoes. She'd been on cloud nine since the other night with Roman and it was going to take more than the bottom of Nadia's pumps to bring her down. She couldn't wait for their dinner tonight to gush over the details of her date with Roman. For the first time being with him, he was present. "It was so... different. He was different."

"Well, you wanted changed behavior. That's the best apology," Brielle smirked, enjoying her bowl of fruit. Brielle sat with her legs crossed in the armchair that sat off in the corner of Wren's office. She was relaxed without two kids hanging off of her, demanding her attention.

The smile from Wren's date hadn't faded in the least. Roman was ever present in the front of her mind since the last time she saw him. There were tiny pieces of her that didn't want to believe that he was changing into the man she wanted and needed but his actions were speaking volumes.

Leaning back in her office chair, she looked over at Nadia, who was pecking away on the screen of her phone. As she smiled at her friends, her greatest fear loomed over her, that this feeling would be short-lived and, in a week, they'd be back to being estranged. "Why are you in your head about this, Wren? Get out. Everything is going the way you wanted then, finally. What's the worry?"

"That he's going to back step," Brielle answered Nadia's question with a mouth full of fruit. "I live with that fear every day, but I can't let it affect us moving forward and you shouldn't let it stop you either."

"You're right," Wren muttered, clamping down on her lip. Just as Brielle was lifting her finger to start her response, a soft knock graced the office door. "Come in."

"Hey, Wren," her office assistant popped her head in the office and smiled. "You have someone here to see you."

Wren frowned and glanced at her schedule that was open on her laptop. "I don't have any meetings."

"You don't, but I think you might want to take this impromptu meeting," her smile widened as Wren gave in. Brielle and Nadia started to gather their things so Wren could handle her business.

"I have to go anyway. Kwame is about to blow our budget out the damn roof," Nadia groaned, tossing her bag over her shoulder. "We're still on for dinner, tonight, right?"

"Yes," Brielle and Wren answered together.

"I am child-free, so I'm going to take advantage of it,"

Brielle added, slipping her feet back into her sandals. "I'll see you tonight."

As Brielle and Nadia exited the office, Roman walked in with flowers in one hand and food in the other. As if she wasn't smiling big enough, it grew wider making her eyes disappear behind her cheeks. "What are you doing here?"

"I was in the area," he smirked softly, placing the food down on the desk.

Wren kissed her teeth and bit down on her lip, again. The sight and scent of Roman made her want to jump his bones here and now. His fitted white tee against his toasted caramel ink covered skin made her lick her lips. She remembered the taste of his skin and she loved the contrast of her chocolate skin against his. As she stood up, she clenched her thighs together and grunted lowly.

A low sigh reset her focus and she released her lip from her teeth. "In the area? I highly doubt that, but you're here, so I'll take it."

"All play and no work, I see," he smirked, stepping around the desk and pulling her into his arms. Roman placed a soft kiss to her cheek and pulled back, feeling his dick stiffen in his pants.

"Brielle is kid-free and Nadia is trying not to go to jail for homicide."

"Well, I'm glad you're free. I missed you." The rumble of his baritone in her ear made her moan. They wanted each other, desperately. But neither of them wanted to take a premature step and damage what they were trying to build together.

Wren wasn't sure how much longer she could be in his presence and keep her hands off of him. "Let's eat."

"I can eat," Roman let a devilish smirk cross his face as he grunted, looking over her. Wren wore a black dress that hugged her curves and dipped low in the back. Watching her walk away made his dick stiffen more. Adjusting his pants quickly, he met her on the other side of the desk and opened the bag of food.

"You're nasty, you know that?" Wren's lustful glare over her shoulder was making it very hard for him to be in a room with her and keep his hands to himself. Her eyes, her scent, being in her warmth was all overwhelming. If he was going to make it through this impromptu lunch with his pants up, he needed to be far away from her.

"Chinese... I meant. I could eat the Chinese."

"I hope you got my favorite," she hummed, brushing against him.

It was becoming almost impossible not to touch her. "What's your favorite?"

Placing a kiss to the back of his neck, she ran her hands down the front of his body until she reached the waist of his pants. "You're my favorite."

"Wren," Roman groaned, taking her hand in his and kissing her knuckles. A nervous chuckle left his lips and he handed Wren her container of house lo mein and stepped off to the side. "You... girl."

"What?" She was on him like a skin. "Just relax, baby."

Roman was used to Wren having her way and this wasn't any different than any other times before. She had him aroused and when she wanted it, she took it. Dropping to her knees, she unfastened his belt buckle while holding eye contact with Roman. She couldn't get him free quick enough because his rod was now standing at attention, waiting for her to hungrily take him into her mouth.

The warmth of her mouth caused him to tense up and release a deep-throated groan. "Shit."

Wren placed her hands around his hips to hold him

steady while she gave him the best head to date. Roman braced himself against the desk with his left hand while his right gripped the root of her hair. Her moans were making the rest of his blood rush down. If she kept this up, he was going to explode without warning.

Wren slurped, bobbed and rotated his balls in her hands. She knew that it was a sure way to make him tense, explode and then relax. Since he dropped her off the other night, all she could think about was pleasing him.

"Fuck," Roman groaned while Wren used her hands to get the results she wanted. His cream ran down her tongue. Soon enough, her labor had yielded the results she wanted. She didn't miss a drop, she moaned and looked up at Roman attempting to put himself back together.

Once every drop was gone, she kissed the tip, licked her lips and stood back to her feet. Roman grunted while straightening himself. "You know you're going to pay for this right?"

"That's the goal," Wren smirked, fixing her dress, picking up her container of food and sitting behind her desk. "Let's eat."

"She's been on that phone since we got here," Brielle groaned, looking over her shoulder and watching Nadia pace the sidewalk outside the restaurant. "This job is more stressful than her first one."

"No, that's my brother driving her up the damn wall."

"You think that maybe we can somehow force them together?" Brielle asked with a devilish smile, twirling her straw around her drink.

"Brielle," Wren chuckled shaking her head. "I don't

want to be in that mix. Because when it hits the fan, and with Nadia and Kwame it *will* hit the fan, I don't want any shit on me. If that's what you want to do, more power to you."

"I'm just saying they've been at each other's throats since forever. You can't tell him it's because they really like each other."

"Mmm," Wren raised her brow. "You could possibly be on to something. Maybe throw the bait at the cookout this weekend."

"See! I knew you would hop on. That would be perfect. Especially since you and Roman are back on good terms," Brielle clapped her hands together and smiled.

"If it blows up, it's on you, though," Wren shook her head and watchedo Nadia stop and flail her arms in the air before ending the call. "She might need a strong ass drink when she gets in here."

"Or two," Brielle added before Nadia returned the table. "You good?"

"I am great," Nadia forced a smile, waving the bartender down. "So... Wren, did you and Roman tear the office up."

"We didn't but I can promise you he hasn't stopped thinking about me since he walked out."

"Oh, shit," Brielle grinned and Nadia popped her brow up. "Girl, get your man!"

"Oh, baby. I got him."

*N*adia Garrett

ONE LAST GLANCE IN THE MIRROR GAVE NADIA THE self-assurance she needed before stepping out of the house. With all the work she had on her plate, she didn't want to be at Julian and Brielle's cookout. She'd rather get a handle on both of the fires going on at the restaurant. One fire being the delay of the supplies she needed to complete her portion of work and the other being balancing the remainder of the budget.

Kwame had conveniently gone M.I.A, which was causing her a great deal of anxiety. The fate of Isabella's culinary career rested in their hands and Kwame couldn't even bother to show up to work. Praying silently that she didn't feel the urge to step to Kwame about his recent bull-shit because they had enough blow ups in group settings, she didn't want today to be another issue.

Once she arrived at the Harris', she grabbed the dish off

the passenger seat and headed into the house. Roman and Julian were by the girls, drinking beer and chatting. Brielle and Wren were putting the final touches on the food going out to the table on the patio and Kamaiyah was playing with the babies. "Hey!"

"Damn, you tell black people to show up at two and they show up at three," Brielle kissed her teeth before smiling at Nadia.

"I'm sorry. Kwame didn't submit the numbers to the accountant last week so I was caught doing that," she shared with a sigh and pushed her hair out of her face. "What can I help with?"

"Help me with the plates and cups and we can eat. We are not waiting for Kwame to show up," Brielle replied walked out the kitchen.

Wren looked over her shoulder to make sure Brielle was gone before turning to Nadia. "Everything with Kwame seems normal, right?"

"Not necessarily. Is everything okay?"

"I don't know. I'll figure it out."

Nadia chose not to delve any further into it. Instead, she stacked the cups and plates on top of the dish she was carrying and walked out to the patio. She would be lying to say that she didn't feel like something with Kwame was off. She'd been around him long enough to know if something wasn't right. But Kwame wasn't her issue and she couldn't tell if all was well until she laid her eyes on him.

An hour into the cookout, he finally walked in, with a guest. "I didn't mention bringing a plus one," Brielle muttered, looking over her red solo cup at Kwame holding the hand of a very pretty brown skin woman.

"Damn, she's fine," Nadia grunted, shaking her head.

Wren's eyes grew wide along with Julian and Roman's. "What in the entire fuck?"

"What?" Nadia and Brielle asked in unison.

"That's his ex," Wren mumbled. "The one who broke his heart... What the hell is he doing here with her?"

"Probably because she's fine," Nadia shrugged, feeling a tinge of jealousy in her gut. It was unfamiliar and she didn't like it. Shaking off the feeling, she poured herself a drink and went back to eating her food.

"Kwame," Julian greeted him with a hug. Pulling away and looking at his date, Julian forced a smile. "Keisha, how you been?"

"I've been great. You look good," Keisha returned, making Brielle, Nadia and Wren twist their faces. Julian could feel the heat coming from the table. Nervously chuckling, he stepped off after patting Kwame's shoulders.

"This is cute." Keisha looked around the landscape of the backyard and smiled. Her smile and presence made everyone who knew who she was cringe.

Roman looked at Kwame oddly before shifting his eyes over to Keisha and nodding his head, acknowledging her. "Listen, the ladies are behind you at the table. You remember Brielle, Julian's wife. My lady, Wren and that's Nadia and my baby sister is lying down inside."

Wren shot Roman a look as Keisha turned around and smiled at them. "Kwame, come help me with these ribs."

Before Kwame could protest, Roman was pushing him inside the house while Brielle and Wren just stared at Keisha like she had seven eyes.

"Brielle, your home is beautiful."

"Mm, thanks," Brielle muttered, drinking the rest of the contents in her cup.

"Hello, Keisha," Wren smirked. "I got to ask... Why are you here with my brother? Haven't you done enough?"

Nadia leaned back in her seat and looked back at them. "Wren, can't we just let the past be the past?"

"Fucking every man in town was the past? Oh, okay. I didn't know hoe tendencies died so easily. Have your way," Wren shrugged her shoulders as Nadia's eyes popped open. She pushed herself from the seat and traveled inside the house.

Nadia looked at Keisha and smiled. "So, you're the one that's been occupying all his time? Hmmm... I can see why he'd neglect his responsibilities for a week."

"You know how the days following an overdue reunion can go," Keisha smiled, making Brielle roll her eyes in disgust.

Nadia's eyebrows rose and she pursed her lips together. "Nah. No. I actually can't say that I do."

JULIAN HARRIS

"WHY THE HELL IS KEISHA HERE?" WREN ASKED, breaking through the guys' huddle in the kitchen. "You don't remember how she tore up your life the first time? You needed another crash course?"

"I was just asking him that," Roman parroted, folding his arms over his chest and leaning back on the counter. "I don't think this is a good idea."

"Kwame is a grown ass man. If he wants to fuck up his life, a second time around, let him," Julian groaned, rubbing his brow. Julian's aggravation lie with Kwame's inability to make a sound decision but he saw this situation exploding in his face again. "You know that's where it's going right?"

"Why are y'all riding me so hard? It's not like that this time around," Kwame defended.

"We're just trying to save you from getting hurt again because it's clear –"

"It's clear that the bitch threw you some pussy and you lost your damn mind again," Wren cut Roman off, throwing her hands up. "I love you, but this is a mistake."

"Wren, I let you live your life. Please let me live mine," Kwame groaned walking, out the kitchen as Nadia walked in and the doorbell rang.

"But why would you bring her around us when we know what you went through the first time with her?" Wren continued her questioning as Nadia leaned on the counter watching the show. She only walked in for more napkins but now she was in the mix and didn't want to get out of it.

Kwame cut his eyes over at Nadia, who looked pleased by all of this. "What you got to say?"

"Actually, I have nothing to say, Kwame. It's your life, your sanity or the lack thereof, and your heart. You can make a mess of it if you want to, but you're the only one responsible for picking up the pieces when the dust settles. I mean, if you ask me... you could've done better."

The doorbell steadily rang and no one bothered to move to get it. Instead, everyone was consumed with Kwame and the worst move he's made, by far. "I guess I need to get that."

"I guess you do," Roman shrugged his shoulders. "It's your house."

"You need to talk to him," Wren fussed, looking up at Roman ignoring Julian's remark to answer his own doorbell.

"Baby, what am I supposed to do about it?" Roman

asked, going back and forth with Wren as if Kwame wasn't standing right there. Kwame was now quiet after hearing Nadia's take on all of this. He exhaled sharply and tightened his jaw.

Julian pulled the door open and looked down at Keera standing on the other side. "Are you going to let me in?"

"Nah," Julian forced through his teeth and blocked the door. "Where the fuck have you been?"

"I told you I needed some time." Keera shared, furrowing her brow like she was something more to Julian other than just his side chick.

"So, you just dump my kid off and disappear? That's not how this shit works, Keera! Get the fuck out of here." Seeing her again sent Julian through the roof. Somehow, he expected her to be more of a mother than what she was. It was disappointing to know that she could just drop her baby off and run away for the sake of getting herself together.

"That's *our* kid," Keera forcefully corrected, trying to get past Julian.

Julian kissed his teeth and chuckled. "Nah, remember I told you if you weren't back in three months, I was filing for full custody. You're a day late and a dollar short."

"Are you serious?" Her voice rose, alarming Nadia and Wren and causing them to poke their heads out of the kitchen and observe Julian's hiked shoulders.

"Keera, do I look like I'm fucking playing with you? I wasn't blowing smoke when I told you that. Get your ass out of here," Julian pointed over her head. Keera barreled her way past Julian only to be met by Nadia whose face was twisted. Her body language spoke louder than any words exchanged between the former lovers.

Nadia rushed Keera and pushed her back towards the door. "Bitch, are you hard of hearing?"

"Stay out of it. You've done enough," Keera grunted, trying to get Nadia off of her. "I just want my child."

"It looks like I haven't done enough because you're here. I know you heard Julian. You're not getting a damn thing." Nadia wasn't going to let this one go as easily as she did before. She vowed that the next time she saw her, she was going to put her hands on her, and Nadia always kept her word.

"What the hell is going on out here?" Brielle asked, bolting into the house after hearing the commotion from the backyard. Keisha wasn't too far behind her. Although she wasn't going to offer any assistance, she was going to enjoy the show. "I know y'all didn't leave me with that whore... What is this about?"

"Brielle, where's the bathroom?" Roman asked trying to distract Brielle from the commotion at the door. Brielle couldn't ignore the fact the Nadia now had both her hands around Keera's throat and Kwame was rushing past everyone to pull Nadia off of her.

Brielle looked at Roman oddly and continued to the door. Pushing Julian out her way, she stepped behind Nadia to see Keera. "Oh, I've been waiting on you, bitch."

It took all of Kwame's strength to get Nadia off of Keera. By now, they were outside, tumbling down the steps of the house, trying to get Nadia to let go. Wrapping his arms around her waist, he lifted her off her feet, giving Nadia a clear shot at Keera's face with the bottom of her shoe. Kwame whipped her around before she could follow through with kicking Keera in the face. "Let me go, Kwame!"

Her pleas were not heard by Kwame. His grip on her was tight, as she squirmed and tried to get away from him. "I'm going to beat the bitch's ass. Let me go!"

Brielle jogged down the steps and wasted no time slapping Keera across the face. Just as fast as she got down the stairs, Wren followed her but Roman snatched her up before she could touch the bottom step.

"You will not even think about it," Roman sternly spoke in Wren's ear. "Y'all will kill that girl."

"That's the point, Roman!" Nadia shouted over Kwame's shoulder while still wrestling to get away from him.

"What kind of woman are you? You dump your child off here and have the nerve to show back up, months later, and demand something!" Brielle still had a great amount of anger built up and she took it out on Keera. Julian let her have her way for about two minutes before he separated his wife from his baby momma. "Get off me, Julian! I owe that hoe an ass whooping of a lifetime."

"Get out of here, Keera!" Julian based, pulling Brielle in the house.

Keera reluctantly walked back to her car but not before shouting, "I'll be back. Believe that!"

"Bitch, I wish you would," Nadia spat. "I'll rearrange your entire fucking face!"

Kwame groaned, pinning Nadia to the wall while Keisha stood off in the background, watching how he handled her.

"Look at me," he ordered, trying to hold Nadia steady. "Look at me! Calm your ass down!"

Grudgingly, Nadia focused on Kwame, letting her heaving settle. "What was all that about?" Kwame shook her slightly. "Come on, you're better than that. Breathe... chill out."

Nadia looked at him and removed her arm from his grip,

when she noticed that everyone was watching the two of them.

"You shouldn't worry about it. I'm good. I got it... just like everything else." Nadia stepped out of his grasp and adjusted her dress.

"Julian, you told me that she wouldn't be a problem. I don't want to see her again!" Brielle shouted, climbing the stairs. "Y'all can go home!"

"I'm going to get Kamaiyah," Wren spoke up, walking past Kwame and Keisha, who was glaring at him in disapproval.

What was supposed to be a great evening for friends had turned into an evening of side chicks and unapproved girlfriends. It was all a mess.

"I'm going home," Nadia groaned, grabbing her keys.

"Jesus," Roman groaned, smacking his forehead. "What the hell was all of that?"

"I don't know," Kwame huffed, watching Nadia walking out.

Keisha's eyes narrowed, irritated by how consumed he was with her. "Kwame take me home. Now!"

"I'll catch up with you boys later. I gotta go put this fire out," Julian shook his head, shaking Roman and Kwame's hands before climbing the stairs behind Brielle. "Unbelievable."

16

ROMAN DANIELS

After Nadia made her dramatic exit, Kwame and Keisha followed suit. Once Wren pulled Kamaiyah away from the babies they headed toward Roman's condo. The ride was silent and Roman could tell that Wren was in deep thought about everything that transpired over the last hour. Neither of them expected the day to take a quick turn.

"I wish, I would've eaten more," Kamaiyah mumbled from the back seat. "I'm hungry again."

Roman looked up in the rearview mirror and looked at her. "What do you want?"

"I'll order pizza, just take me home," Kamaiyah replied leaning her head on the window. Roman nodded his head and did exactly what she asked. Once he had Kamaiyah settled inside of the condo, he traveled back down to the car to take Wren home.

Roman placed his hand on her thigh, hoping that she'd wrap her hand around his. She didn't budge, she stared out the window with her chin propped on her knuckles. Letting a light sigh exit his lips, he continued the ride in silence. Reaching her apartment building, he parked the car and sat in Wren's silence. He would sit here all night until she was ready to talk.

The sound of the looming car engine relaxed Wren's mind. The longer she listened to it hum along with the music that played softly, her shoulders relaxed. Finally, she'd taken his hands in hers and released a heavy sigh. "I cannot believe that she showed back up."

"Keera or Keisha?" Roman asked, looking at the steering wheel. He knew that both Julian and Kwame were getting an ear full. Julian's ears were bleeding from Brielle's temper while Keisha was going on about how he couldn't keep his hands to himself. "I can't believe y'all tagged that girl like that. I knew y'all didn't play about each other but that was some next level shit."

"Shit, both. How could Kwame be so stupid to let her

back in?" Wren asked, looking at him. "She broke him so bad. If she does it again, he won't be the same, and I will always ride for them. That's not even a question."

Wren's love for her brother and her girls ran deep. Sometimes deeper than she let on. Underneath Kwame's tough exterior was a tender, loving being that wanted love just as much as the rest of them. But, if he spent any more time with Keisha, that tender soul would harden.

"He's going to be fine, babe," Roman spoke up, kissing her knuckles. "Trust me. He will wake up soon enough. You didn't see how he handled Nadia? He forgot all about Keisha."

"Shit, I hope so," Wren muttered. Sighing and slouching down into the seat, she placed her feet on the dashboard. "Those two... I wonder when they're going to wake up and just seal the deal. They are gasoline and fire."

"That might be a good or a bad thing. They could be really good for each other or they could do some serious damage," Roman pointed out, staring at the dashboard of his car.

"How's Kamaiyah? She hasn't been as mouthy as usual." Wren looked over at him and admired his face underneath the light of the moon.

"Morning sickness and figuring out what her next step is. I gave her a job down at the shop so she can have insurance and some sort of income."

Wren smirked softly, looking at Roman with soft eyes of admiration. "You have really surprised me."

"What do you mean?"

Releasing his hand and rubbing his chin with the back of her hand, she hummed. "You're a man. The man you fought so hard to ignore."

"I wasn't ignoring him, per se... I was scared, if I'm being honest."

"Scared of what?"

"Ending up being like my pops and being so caught up in the fast life that I would lose myself and my family. I was so afraid of breaking your heart that, while I was distancing myself trying to save it, I broke it anyway."

"What made you want to change? You know, besides me?" Wren mentioned, playfully batting her eyelashes, making Roman smirk.

"Kamaiyah."

He closed his eyes and thought about that overwhelming feeling of uncertainty when he returned to Compton to get her. "When I went back to get her, we had a conversation and I asked her why she would choose someone like that nigga she found herself wrapped up in. And she told me that she thought she was supposed to choose someone who was inconsistent and an all-around fuck nigga because that's all we showed her. Pops couldn't show her any better but I had to change. There was no way around it. When she looks at me, she has to see the man she's supposed to want, if that makes sense. Senior ain't here to set the tone for her, so that weight lies on my shoulders."

Kissing his cheek, she smiled tenderly at him. "I'm happy you did. I missed you."

Roman smiled and kissed her lips affectionately. "I missed you."

"You want to come in?"

"Yeah, sure."

Roman got out of the car and grabbed his duffle bag from the trunk. "You always keep an overnight bag?" Wren asked, getting out the car.

"It's my gym bag. I always keep clean clothes in my gym

bag," he chuckled as Wren rolled her eyes and mmhmm'd him. "What do you want it to be?"

"Just making sure you ain't creeping."

"I'm always creeping on your fine ass. Let's go inside."

Following her up the stairs to her apartment and inside, he watched as she removed her sandals and walked down the hall. "I am so tired."

Roman smirked to himself, thinking about holding her in his arms while she slept peacefully. "Let's lay down."

"Let's?" Wren smirked and hiked her eyebrow. "Like let us?" She was in the business of toying with Roman and his emotions. "You can have the guest bedroom. Don't get any slick ideas either."

"Yo, are you serious?" Roman frowned his face, placing his hand on his chest.

Wren turned on her heels and untied the string of her halter sundress. Letting it fall around her ankles, she bent over to pick it up and walked into her room. She was doing any and everything to tease him. All she was doing was writing a check that she would have to eventually cash. "Dead serious. Good night. I'll see you in the morning."

Closing the door, Roman stood in the hallway with a full erection and a bewildered look on his face. For the night, he would cool himself off. But, when the morning came, he would make her pay for it dearly.

Walking into the guest bedroom, he sat on the edge of the bed and set the alarm at the condo because Kamaiyah could never remember to do it. Kwame's name flashed on the screen. Silently thanking God for the distraction, he answered the phone and dropped back into the pillows. "Mr. Keisha."

"Don't play with me, nigga." Kwame kissed his teeth

through the phone and groaned. "What was all that shit y'all were giving me about it?"

"If you have to ask me, I got a feeling that you already know." Roman chuckled.

"It's not like that, this time around."

"You sound like you're trying to convince yourself more than me, nigga. And you sound stupid as hell. Wren is really worried about you." Roman informed him. "And what was all that shit with you and Nadia?"

Kwame sighed. "This girl got a fucking hold on me. I can't break that shit."

"Which one? Because you were definitely caught up for a minute. What are you running from?"

"What I got to run from?"

"Yourself, nigga. And the truth. Listen, I'm not going to tell you what you already know. But what I do know is your soft ass better not come around crying when she fucks you up. Don't find yourself somewhere you have no business being."

"I'm not talking to you no more." Kwame groaned before hanging up on Roman.

"Nigga, you called me." Roman chuckled. "That nigga is confused as hell."

AFTER SHOWERING, ROMAN STEPPED OUT OF THE guest bedroom to see Wren's door still closed. Dialing Kamaiyah's number, he shuffled into the kitchen and started looking for something to cook for breakfast. Surely, the smell of food would coax her out of the room. Once he had her out, he could have his way. She was going to pay dearly for her antics the past week.

"Ah," he cheered, pulling out the bacon, eggs and bread to prepare a breakfast made for champs.

"Hey, Ro," Kamaiyah tiredly answered. "Before you start your twenty-one questions, I am okay. Yes, I've eaten. No, I don't need anything. Enjoy your time with Wren, I'm going to sleep. I love you."

"I love you, too. I'll see you when I get home." Ending their call, he turned around to see Wren standing at the entrance of the kitchen, in one of his old t-shirts.

"How'd you sleep?" Wren's smirk was sly, as she inched the t-shirt up her thighs.

"How you think I slept?" Roman asked her, closing the space between the two with his lip clamped between his teeth. not taking his eyes off her chocolate covered thighs.

He placed his hands on her thighs and pulled the shirt up over her head. "Like a baby."

"You think you got me by the balls, huh?" He grunted, lifting her right leg up and placing his middle finger in her mouth. "I got to give it to you... you damn near drove me crazy."

Wren sucked his finger and released it from her mouth. Running his finger from her lips down her body to her center, he parted her petals and inserted his finger inside of her folds. Wren's back arched and she bit down on her lip. Roman loved the ecstasy that was flooding into her face. Her nectar was dripping over his finger and all over his knuckles.

"Ro," she moaned and tried to look at him with hooded eyes. "Baby."

He chuckled lowly, feeling her body tense up. Removing his finger from her folds, he placed it in his mouth and groaned. "Shit, you taste good."

Picking her up, he pushed her further up the wall so she

could wrap her legs around his neck. Her flower was front and center to his lips and Roman couldn't wait to indulge in his meal. He was going to drive her crazy. He groaned while his tongue craved the taste of her. Running its thickness over her bud, Wren's moans were growing louder. Her river was flowing and soaking his face. "Shit, you taste good."

"Shit, Ro— fuck! I'm going to cum."

"Let that shit go," he groaned, holding her up while she came on command. Wren was posted on the wall like a painting while Roman continued to make her pay for every moment she teased him.

"I'm going to make you beg me to stop."

"Shit!"

 ren Franklin

THEY MADE A MESS IN THE KITCHEN; BROKEN EGGS ON the floor, broken vases from the counter and their contents of sugar and flour spread across the apartment to the bedroom. Wren dug her nails into his back while he slow stroked her, continuously hitting her g-spot. Her eyes rolled to the back of her head and she was unable to speak any more. It was an overwhelming sense of euphoria. Every nerve, every sense, every inch of her body was heightened. Her eyes were clamped shut as she explored the heavens and all the goodness that God had to offer. Roman's full, succulent lips pressed against her skin, while he made sweet love to her, only added to her pleasure.

"Stop teasing me," she moaned in his ear, damn near begging him to take her to the edge. Roman refused. He was very serious when he said that she was going to regret teasing him. "Baby, please."

"Don't tell me what to do," he groaned, gripping her thighs. "You didn't give my shit away, did you?"

"Baby," Wren moaned, trying to answer him but she couldn't.

"Did you?"

"No," she whimpered, digging her nails in his back more. "You feel so fucking good."

Tongue kissing her sensually, she moaned into his mouth, wrapping herself around him tighter. With every kiss and every stroke, she became wetter, making it an honor to swim through her sea. Soon, Roman had had enough of teasing her and pushed her legs from around him and spread them wide. He picked up his speed, making her hum, groan, moan, grunt and curse his name. Diving deeper inside, he felt himself climbing his mountain. Judging by the way her walls tightened around him, she was almost there.

Being the gentleman that he was, he made sure that she got hers before he tagged her walls with his graffiti. "Mmm... shit," Wren moaned, running her hands down his abs.

Refusing to leave her home, her warmth and her garden, he covered her lips with his and groaned against them. "You know you're mine, right?"

"Mmhmm," Wren couldn't manage to utter a word. She was riding her starburst of euphoria.

Wren rolled over to her stomach and passed out, once Roman pulled out. Traveling to the bathroom he watched as she slept peacefully. Once he cleaned up, he went to clean up their mess and ordered lunch. Leaving the house meant that he would have to share her with the outside world. He wasn't ready to share yet and he still wasn't done with her.

Checking his phone, he saw a message from Nadia letting him know that she was going to get Kamaiyah and hang out with her for the rest of the day. He texted her back thanking her. Nadia was always good like that. He and the rest of the group wanted her to have something solid, too, but he wasn't going to go as far as trying to set her up. He could only pray that she and Kwame could drop the act before it was too late and settle their differences, once and for all.

He checked in on the shop before hearing Wren's bedroom door open. Peeking down the hall, he smiled at her relieved expression. "I thought you left me," reaching him, she wrapped her arms around his waist and kissed his bare chest.

"Come on," Roman kissed his teeth slightly. "Look at me."

Wren dragged her eyes from the floor to Roman's almond eyes staring down at her. He could look at her and pick up on her fears. He was in tune with her and it was beautiful. He found it amazing what could happen when he let his guard down and loved without fear of failing her.

"I'm not going nowhere, not even if you make me. I've had enough of that running and inconsistent shit. I wasn't talking last night just to hear myself talk. You hear me?"

Wren bit her lip and nodded her head. "You know you're my man, now, right?"

"Mission accomplished," he muttered against her lips. "You want to eat before I bend you over?"

"Oh, yes," she giggled. "We got to play catch up."

Smacking her ass, he grinned devilishly. "We sure do. Go sit down."

KWAME FRANKLIN

. . .

KEISHA'S STARE WAS UNAVOIDABLE AT THIS POINT. Kwame had tried his best to ignore it all day, but she wasn't going to let go of it. He told her, time after time, that Nadia was nothing but a business associate. He told himself, time after time, that they just did business together, there was nothing else lying beneath the surface. But Keisha believed that Kwame had unspoken feelings for her, especially with the way he handled her the other day.

"Keisha," Kwame groaned, sitting on the couch with his feet propped up on the table. "I'm not doing this with you again."

"I am not going through this with you again. I know how this ends up."

"And how does it end up, Keisha?" He did not want to have any conversation with Keisha about Nadia. There was nothing to talk about. Or so he told himself.

Keisha growled lowly at his response before she stood in front of him. "That you're going to slip and fall dick first into her pussy. That's what is going to end up happening. Watch. You say she's nothing, but you handle her like she means something to you."

"I've known her since college, we work together. Like what the fuck you want me to do? I am not going to sit here and defend this over and over again," Kwame fussed.

"Do you or do you not care for her?"

He rolled his eyes and slouched deeper into the couch. "Keisha! And if I did, then what?"

Keisha folded her arms across her body and grunted. "If you did, dead it."

Kwame dropped his head back and began to laugh. Standing to his feet, he grabbed his beer and walked outside, away from her. "You got to be out your damn mind. You are not walking into my house and demanding shit out of me. She's been around longer than you. You are not going to try to remove shit from my life."

"See what I'm saying. You're defending her, which means it's more. I will not be fighting for your attention."

Kwame was quickly reminded of why their relationship ended years ago. "You don't have to."

"So, you're going to get rid of her?" Keisha smirked with satisfaction as Kwame turned around and stroked the side of her face with his index finger.

"No," he whispered with a smile. "I'm getting rid of you. You can see yourself out."

Stepping away, he traveled the far side of the pool and looked out into the distance. The truth had shown up and slapped him in the face.

"Fuck," he released after hearing Keisha walk away. "What the fuck am I going to do about this shit, now?"

Digging into his pocket, he pulled out his phone and dialed his father's number, dropping his body into the pool chair. "Big man!" Terry answered the phone in a happy tone. "What's going on?"

"Big dog," Kwame replied rubbing his temple. "I think you might be right."

"About that tender little thing that you're spending time with every day?"

"Nadia... Yes."

"Tell me what happened?" he imagined Terry to be sitting in his favorite chair with his legs crossed, eating his nuts with a smirk on his face.

"Pops, stop smirking," Kwame chuckled, dropping his head back. "So, some shit went down yesterday, and it was a natural instinct for me to protect her and Keisha was there and that turned into a big ass thing. You know that girl had the nerve to ask me to choose."

"Oh, no," Terry gasped, easing Kwame's frustration.

He couldn't help but laugh. "Nah, pops, it's nothing. I don't have the time nor the patience to deal with her ass."

"But look at you. Son, all jokes aside. Knock her up."

"I am really about to hang up on your ass, man. I will not. I know I'm your son and all but there's just some shit I will not be doing."

"Bet all that aggression you had when you called is gone. Now, if what you are unconsciously feeling is for real, you should probably feel it out. See if it's reciprocated."

"Hmm... We'll see."

"I can't wait to see what you end up doing. You're my son, so I have an idea."

"Why did I even call your ignorant ass?" Kwame laughed, palming his face. "You have no chill."

"I sure don't. And you sounded like you needed a laugh. I don't know why the hell you would get back with that rabid ass girl."

"Small lapse in judgment. Won't catch me slipping again."

"Yeah, and pigs are flying."

"You know what...? Bye."

18

*N*adia Garrett

THERE WAS A LOT ABOUT KAMAIYAH THAT REMINDED Nadia of herself when she was seventeen. She remembered feeling like no one saw her or was willing to hear her. The least she could do was pull her out of the house and make sure she was okay.

"You're pretty," Kamaiyah spoke up, looking at Nadia from across the table. "Why are you single? Most of the pretty girls always get chosen by the good guys first. Plus, you're in LA, so I'm so confused. Are you crazy?"

"Yes," Nadia laughed. "I am crazy but that's not why I'm single."

"Then, what is it?" Kamaiyah asked as Nadia chewed on the inside of her cheek.

"Whew, chile. Where do I start?" Nadia asked leaning up on her elbows. "When I was twelve, I was... raped by a family friend, until I was sixteen. When my mom found out, I was called every name in the book by her and the guys in my neighborhood. It put a bad taste in my mouth. And I really didn't trust anyone. I also didn't have any siblings to look out for me, so I just stayed to myself."

"Shit," Kamaiyah groaned. "Here I am thinking that my situation was bad. Franco just didn't want to do the right thing. He wanted the street life more than he wanted a life with me. I guess, in some ways, I'm really happy that my mom lost her shit and called Roman... what happened to your baby?"

"I lost it," Nadia shared before smiling faintly. "I know all of this seems like it's a burden, but you're surrounded by people who love you and want the best for you. Count your blessings and take it a day at a time."

"Damn," Kamaiyah shook her head. "How did you get over all of that?"

"Honestly? I'm still healing wounds. But, every day that I get up, I make a choice to move forward. You get to a point where moping around stops working, being angry isn't useful and playing the victim is pathetic. In life, we all go through some shit. It's how we handle that shit that makes us strong. Right now, you are doing one of the most amazing things that you will ever do and that's give life. Sure, how you got here sucks. Sure, Franco is an asshole but it's about how Kamaiyah comes through this. When you look back on this, what do you want to say?"

"I want to say, damn, I made it," Kamaiyah smiled slightly. "If you made it through all of that, and you're a boss, I know I can do it. Thank you for taking me out today. I get bored sitting in the house. School sucks."

"You'll be out of there before you know it. I want you to know that your brother and the rest of us are proud of you and if you need anything, I'm always here for you. Don't feel like you're invisible or unwanted because that's so far from the truth. So, promise me that when you get in your head, you'll call one of us," Nadia held her pinky out.

"You're corny," Kamaiyah giggled before wrapping her pinky around Nadia's. "Thank you so much. You have no idea how much this means to me."

"I can only imagine." Nadia winked at her. "Our food is coming, I'm starving."

Julian Harris

After two and a half days, Brielle was finally calm enough to have a conversation and not look at him crazy. Since the cookout had gone wrong, Julian needed to catch up with the guys and go over the events of everything. Sitting in Roman's living room with his feet kicked up, he looked at Kwame who was consumed with his phone.

"Get your feet off my damn table, boy," Roman knocked his feet down before sitting down and kicking his feet up on the table.

"You tripping," Julian kissed his teeth, putting his feet back up.

"You don't pay for nothing around here, homeboy. You got rules in your house, I got rules in my house, too." Roman sassed making Julian roll his eyes. "Kwame, you checking in with Keisha?"

"Fuck you," Kwame groaned from behind his phone. "I'm actually catching up with work, thanks. And, if you must know, I got rid of her ass."

Both Roman and Julian sat up and looked at him. "Stop playing."

"I look like I'm playing, nigga? I am not about to have a headache behind no woman and being controlled about no decision I make. She tried me and she had to go. Simple," Kwame shared before putting his phone down.

Julian raised his brow and stared at him. "Nah. There is something more than that. I know what it is."

"Oh, she was .38 hot about Kwame handling Nadia the other day. I caught that look of disapproval from a mile away."

"I got a hundred bucks saying that she asked him to choose her over Nadia. And Kwame, being the nigga that can't express how he feels about a certain someone, said hell nah." Julian added to Roman's account of events.

Kwame rolled his eyes and kicked his feet up, just to spite Roman. "Since y'all niggas know everything else, ain't no need for me to say shit else."

Julian and Roman looked at each other and smirked before turning back to Kwame. "I knew it! I knew it! I knew it!" Roman shouted, jumping up to his feet. "How long you been feeling Nadia?"

"Nigga, I don't know. Would you sit your simple ass down?"

"Nah! You been walking around here like you don't give a shit about that girl and you done caught feelings!"

"Roman, you are loud," Julian groaned, covering his ears.

"And wrong." Kwame sighed. "Loud and wrong. I didn't say I caught feelings. I might just care a little bit more than I thought."

"Boy," Julian groaned. "You are the worst. Are you just going to sit on this until someone else swoops in and tames her ass? Then, you're going to be walking around all in your damn feelings. I say you tell her."

"Look, big bird. Don't everybody wear their feelings on their sleeve like you," Kwame kissed his teeth. "I am not telling that girl a damn thing."

"That's what your mouth says," Roman grunted, not believing a word Kwame was saying. "That's why his eyes are brown. He's full of shit."

"Fuck you," Kwame groaned.

"Fuck yourself. Nadia Garrett ain't nothing to be taken lightly. You see how she almost round housed Keera, in a damn dress and heels? I can only imagine what she'll do to your hoe ass," Julian snickered, making Kwame and Roman look at him with their brow raised.

"Nigga, you had a whole other bitch. Don't say shit about me being a hoe. You had a wife and a side chick. A janky ass one at that," Kwame corrected him. "You got some nerve. Furthermore, I know who I am and I know who she is. That is a broken heart that I will *not* be responsible for."

"So, you're not going to say shit to her?" Roman frowned. "That's going to be damn near impossible."

"Why?" Kwame frowned.

"Because Julian is a snitching ass nigga!" Roman pointed at Julian who threw his shoe at him in return. "Get your big ass shoe away from me."

"Shut your ass up," Julian groaned. "It doesn't have nothing to do with me snitching. It has everything to do with you opening Pandora's box. Those feelings are about to take over your damn life. Your black ass is going to tell me I'm right and your snitching ass is going to owe me a g. He's going to be in love in three months."

"Kwame don't do love."

"Kwame is a liar," Julian scoffed. "Nose gonna be wide open."

"It be your own friends hating on you." Kwame sighed, rolling his eyes and picking his phone back up.

"We already in the club. You can't ever get in," Roman snickered. "I hope Nadia gives your ass a run."

"And I hope Wren says no to your proposal."

"Whoa," Roman pinned his brows together. "I haven't even talked to Terry."

"Ain't no need to talk to that ignorant ass nigga. It's a go from me." Kwame smirked at Roman. "You sure you ready for that?"

"Listen, I know what it's like not to have that woman in my life. Ain't no damn way I'm going another day without making it official."

Julian smiled and leaned forward to dap Roman. "Look who grew up."

"That's big shit," Kwame dapped him before leaning back in the chair. "You can't fuck this up. When are you doing it?"

"I don't know yet." Roman twirled the ring box in his hand.

"Do it at the restaurant opening, in a couple of weeks. She won't be expecting that shit."

"You know you're up next, right?" Julian glanced over at Kwame who rolled his eyes and looked back at his phone.

"You need to stop wishing ill on me like that. That's rude and God don't like ugly."

"Then, both you niggas need to get out my house then," Roman spoke up.

"Fuck you!" Julian and Kwame said in unison.

oman Daniels

"WHAT IS THAT?" ROMAN ASKED PLACING HIS HANDS on Wren's waist and kissing the base of her neck. "Smells good."

"Stir fry. Kamaiyah wanted it, so I delivered," Wren was loving being consumed with Roman and Kamaiyah. She had to give it to Roman, he wasn't playing when he said he needed a month. They were only a few weeks into his offer and Wren knew that she was sold. She was wrapped in love and it looked good on her. Love that was filling, satisfying and consistently present.

With one final kiss to the neck, Roman hummed. "Remind me to keep her around then. If I'm going to get fed like this every day."

"Every day?" Wren looked over her shoulder at him. "Don't get spoiled. You can cook, too, sir."

"No," Kamaiyah shook her head with disgust. "I want to stay alive. So, Wren, it's all or nothing."

"You drive a hard bargain."

"I do. I like good food, so you're stuck," Kamaiyah replied to Wren. "If you love me like you say you do, don't let him anywhere near those pots."

"I swear, everyone has been hating on me. First Kwame and now my own sister," Roman grabbed his chest. "Where is the love?"

"I don't know. How about you scram and go find it?" Kamaiyah sassed as a heavy knock graced the door. "Look how fast God answers prayers."

"Who raised you to be a hater?" Roman asked, walking over to the door and pulling it open. "Ma. What are you doing here?"

"What do you think I'm doing here? To get my daughter."

Roman's face quickly twisted, and his body tightened up. "Ma, what?"

"You heard me. She needs to be at home, with me. Thank you for all you've done but I'm over it and can take it from here," Shelia smirked, inviting herself into Roman's condo. "Oh, you have a guest."

"Hi, I'm Wren. Roman's girlfriend. It's so nice to meet you," Wren smiled, introducing herself. Shelia didn't even look in her direction. Instead, she looked at Kamaiyah, who refused to make eye contact. "Or not."

"Kamaiyah, go get your things," Shelia ordered.

"No, Kamaiyah," Roman ordered, looking at his mother. "You can't put her out, have me come to get her in the middle of the night and want her back because you have a change of heart. What happens when she does something else you don't like? You can't keep kicking her out and coming back for her. She needs stability."

"Roman, I am her mother. Don't you think I know what my child needs?" Shelia fussed as Roman chuckled lowly and shook his head.

"Nah. Honestly, I don't. You don't even know what you need. How the hell can you take care of her and her child if you cannot take care of yourself," Roman pointed out as Shelia's eyes grew larger.

"Excuse me? What?" She blinked fast and tilted her head to the side. "Pregnant? And neither one of you bothered to tell me? What were you going to do? Let her have it?"

"Yeah!" Kamaiyah and Roman spoke up in unison.

"She's a baby her damn self! What does she know about having a baby?"

"Mom, she's seventeen. What are you going to do, make her get an abortion? We're not doing that," Roman finalized, putting his foot down and coming to Kamaiyah's defense.

"I am her mother. I choose what she does and does not do! Who do you think you are, telling me what I do with my child?!"

"I'm the nigga that stepped up, Ma!" Roman based, causing everyone to jump. "I stepped up. I made sure she had food on the table, clothes on her back. I made sure that the house stayed caught up on the mortgage, after Senior died. I did any and everything to make sure that y'all were okay while you drank the money away. That was me."

"Rome," Wren spoke softly, seeing what the back and forth was doing to Kamaiyah. "Just calm down."

"No," he shook his head. "No one is going to tell me to calm down or ask me about why I made the decisions I made. Ma, Kamaiyah will not go back to Compton. Because if she does —"

"If she does, then what?" Shelia continued to go back and forth with her son, standing toe to toe.

Roman shook his head and stepped back. "I'm not doing this with you."

"No, nigga! You got so much to say. Say it."

Roman bit his lip and regained eye contact with his mother. "She will not turn out like you. You have seen so much pain and misery there that you can't see anything else but that. Since Senior died, you have not been the same. You wear that all over. I don't want that for Kamaiyah. I don't want her getting wrapped up in no hood nigga, only to lose him the same way you lost Senior. She doesn't deserve that, Ma. Neither do you."

Roman looked at his mother and saw nothing but sadness in her eyes. "I forgot."

"You forgot what?" He asked her in the softest of voices he possessed.

"I forgot he was gone. You know, today is our anniversary. I got up and baked him a cake and I forgot."

Wren's face softened, seeing Roman wrap his arms around his mother. "Don't cry, ma."

"I forgot," she sobbed into his chest. Roman couldn't remember the last time she cried like this. He could only remember her dropping to her knees, the night she found out about Senior but never after that. Instead of crying, she hardened her exterior and her heart and moved on like it was nothing. She treated Senior being dead like him being locked away in a cell.

"I love you, Ma," Roman hummed in her ear before wiping her face. "No more crying. Let's forget about all of this, eat dinner and smile okay?"

Shelia nodded her head before letting out a heavy sigh. "I am so sorry. I'm so sorry."

"You're good," Roman stepped back so she could wrap her arms around Kamaiyah.

"Come here," she sniffed, wrapping her arms around her daughter. "I love you. I'm sorry."

"It's okay, Mom, I understand. I really want to stay here. It's peaceful." Kamaiyah hugged her back and laid her head on her shoulder.

Wiping the few lone tears from her eyes, Wren turned the food down on the stove and grabbed her wallet and keys. Slipping out the door, she hurried down the street to the bakery on the corner.

"You know you're staying here tonight," Roman didn't give her a chance to object. His word was final. "Sit down."

"Where did your friend go?" Shelia asked looking around.

Roman smirked. "She'll be back. Be nice to her, ma."

"You should. She's going to be your daughter-in-law soon," Kamaiyah smirked over at Roman. "Before you start, I saw the box on your dresser when I accidentally lost my phone in your room."

"Please keep your mouth shut," Roman groaned, pulling plates down from the cabinet. "Seriously, I'm still planning everything so both of you shut it."

"Why does he act like I can't hold water?" Shelia asked looking at Kamaiyah.

Kamaiyah chuckled and looked over at Roman who looked at his mother with a confused expression on his face. "Because you can't."

"You're a snitch, Ma," Roman spoke up. "You don't even know you be snitching when you're snitching."

Shelia kissed her teeth and rolled her eyes. "I get it! I got it! I won't say a word."

"I bet that won't last long," Kamaiyah snickered, while Roman fixed their plates. A few minutes later, Wren walked back in with a cake in her hands and a smile on her face. "Cake!"

"I figured that, whether or not Senior is here, we should still celebrate your anniversary," Wren announced, putting the cake on the counter. Roman smiled at her and motioned for her to sit down.

He didn't know if he could love her more but, with every passing moment, she showed him differently. She constantly went out of her way to make sure that everyone around her was okay and comfortable. If he wondered whether or not he made the right decision, this moment solidified that he did.

 ren Franklin

THE SMILE ON SHELIA'S FACE WAS ENOUGH FOR WREN to know that today had turned around for her. When she walked into the house, guns blazing, Wren's guard automatically shot up. It was a feeling she was all too familiar with. Especially because it reminded her so much of her mother. To this day, her mother hadn't gotten over what Terry had done to her. She allowed the hate she had for him to fester and harden her once beautiful spirit and gentle heart. It had become hard for Wren to talk to her mother because of it. Even harder after Wren explained to her how vital it was to have her father in her life. Her mother could protest it all she wanted but she wasn't going to stagnate her growth anymore because her mother was hurt.

It took Wren a long time to distinguish her personal hurt from everyone else's. Her life had to go on. Holding on to hurt hadn't done her any good.

Cleaning the kitchen, Wren shook the thoughts of her mother off and refocused on the task at hand.

"Wren...?" Looking over her shoulder to see Shelia leaning on the island countertop, she turned around fully. "I wanted to apologize about earlier. I was wrong."

Roman was clearing the table and froze in his tracks to look over at his mother apologizing. "Wrong?"

"Shut up, boy," Shelia waved him off. "I've never seen him with anyone. You must be special."

Wren smiled and looked down before looking up at Roman, who was headed her way. "She is."

"Well, Wren. I'm happy that he has someone to keep him straight. God knows he doesn't listen to me," Shelia yawned and Roman wrapped his hands around Wren's waist.

"I try. He's hard headed sometimes." Wren giggled while Roman whispered something in her ear.

I got your hard head.

"I'll see you two in the morning." Shelia smiled at her son engaged with Wren. She was happy that he found something to hold on to. Even moreso that he was a man of his word. "Good night."

"Night," Wren managed to say between giggles. "Stop it, your mom is here."

"I'm gone!" Shelia shouted from down the hall.

"I'm going home," Wren shared. "Your mom is here."

"What does that have to do with anything?" Roman asked with his lips pressed against her neck. "Thank you for the cake. That made her night."

"It was nothing."

"No. It was because she came in here, guns blazing. She was going to take all of us out," Roman chuckled, leading her from the kitchen to the living room.

Sitting on the couch, she sighed and cuddled up next to him. "That was intense."

"Shelia requires a certain tone sometimes. I feel like shit, though, because I should have known that it was something to do with Senior when she stormed in here like she lost her damn mind. She doesn't usually act up or cry until..."

"Until she reaches a breaking point. Like most of us women," Wren shrugged. "I could never imagine what it feels like to have your husband leave you without saying goodbye. I don't ever want to feel that."

"You won't," Roman assured her. Engulfing her in his arms, he rested his chin on top of her head. "You know I love you."

"I got a feeling you do," she replied, biting down on her lip.

Roman swallowed the lump in his throat and pulled her on his lap. "I love you, Wren. I need you to know that. Every fiber of my being is yours. Even the ones that work on your damn nerves."

"There's a few of those." Smiling wide, she straddled his lap and kissed his lips. "You should know that I love you, too. Thank you for stepping up to the plate and keeping your word."

They spoke no louder than a whisper. Shelia and Kamaiyah were knocked out in the guest bedroom, but they wanted to be sure not to wake either of them up. "I told you I was coming for you."

"I was waiting." Placing tender kisses on his lips, she wrapped her arms around his neck. Running his hands up and down her thighs, he peeked down the hall. "Turn on a movie."

She craved him. When he was close, she could sense

him, when they were miles apart, she leaned her body in his direction. This was love. She knew it. It didn't come easy with him and it hurt like hell, at times, but this was a love of her own. A love that entered her life and knocked her out. Staggering back to her feet, she decided to enter the ring, one last time, with him. Her confidence was low. She didn't know if she could sway with him, dodge his punches, guard her heart, save her face. But when you're in the ring with love, anything could happen. Love could knock you out, if you let it.

Roman's hand traveled up her thighs and moved her panties to the side. Inserting two of his fingers inside of her warmth, she moaned and bit down on his bottom lip. Rotating her hips around his fingers, she fumbled with the band of his sweatpants trying to get his throbbing dick out. Her ecstasy was intensifying, and she needed him inside her quickly. Soon as she had him free, he pulled his fingers from her folds and placed them in her mouth. Guiding her down on him, Wren sucked her juices off his fingers and moaned at her taste. Working her hips around his pulsating rod, she moaned deeper while Roman fumbled with the remote to drown out her moans.

"Shit, girl," he grunted as she bounced up and down on his dick. "Fuck!"

"Say it again," Wren moaned, holding on to his shoulders. "Tell me you love me again."

"I love you," Roman grunted, grabbing her by the root of her hair and pulling her head back to suck on her neck. "This pussy is good."

"It's all yours," Wren moaned, as her body gushed rivers over his. "All yours."

. . .

144

BRIELLE HARRIS

SHE SAT IN THE MIDDLE OF THE FLOOR, FOLDING clothes and sipping a glass of wine. Brielle basked in the silence of having both babies asleep before nine. Since the blow up with Keera, Brielle hadn't said much to Julian. Her aggravation with the whole situation was rearing its ugly head and she was trying her best to avoid taking it out on Julian, so it was better to remain silent.

Julian, on the other hand, wasn't feeling her silence. He knew, first hand, that her growing silent was a problem. Having experienced Brielle's petty fury before, he didn't want to ever experience it again. Walking into the living room, he sat down next to her and started helping her fold clothes.

"I know you're tired," Brielle broke the silence. "I don't want to keep you up."

"Stop it, babe. You're tired, too. You've been dealing with the babies all day, the least I could do is help you out."

She smiled and looked at him. "Before you say anything, I went down to the courthouse today and took care of the Keera issue."

Brielle paused. "She popped up at my job, yesterday, on her bullshit and I had to talk some sense into her. She only wanted Lillian back so she could get child support. I'm not about to have her use my child as a pawn to get money."

"Mm. You chose her."

"And you chose Kyle," Julian responded as Brielle sighed and dropped her head. "But that doesn't have shit to do with our family. Anyone who threatens your security, or our peace, has to go. Period."

"I hear you."

"I know you hear me. Now, get out your feelings and give your man some love," Julian ordered, taking the clothes out her hands. "A hug, something."

"Julian," Brielle groaned while Julian removed the clothes from her hands. "I don't want to be bothered."

"Oh, too bad, Mrs. Harris. I vowed to love, honor, protect and bother you until that day the breath leaves my body," lifting her body up enough to pull her on his lap, he kissed her lips and hummed. "I got to do that again."

Brielle couldn't help but laugh before Julian covered her face in kisses. "I love you, baby momma."

"Love you, baby daddy. Let me finish."

"Nah," he shook his head. "I got that after I get you."

Julian's hands found her bud, causing him to grin like a kid in the candy store. "Tell me no."

"I hate you," she groaned, biting down on her lip. "I have to be up early with the kids. Julian, don't do this."

He couldn't help but chuckle, feeling her warmth under his touch. The more he teased her, the more she squirmed and moaned. "You're getting up when they start crying."

"I intend to. Tomorrow's your day. But, tonight, you're mine. Stop trying to run from me."

"You get on my damn nerves."

"Keep that same energy, Mrs. Harris."

ren Franklin

"So, you met his mother, huh?" Brielle asked, shifting through the racks of clothes. "You think she can fit this?"

Holding up an outfit for Wren to see, she nodded her head. "I'll take it to her."

The girls decided to take Kamaiyah shopping for clothes she would need for work and the duration of her pregnancy. Nadia was already planning her baby shower, and no one was going to object to it. They were truly a tribe, in every sense of the word. When the world threw its bullshit at them, they shielded each other from the blow. That was love. It was pure and rewarding. Anyone coming into this fold had to know that the love these women had for each other was unshakeable.

"I did. At first, I was a little taken aback because of the way she busted in the house, like she owned something. But, as she continued on with her fussing, she reminded me of my mom," Wren started explaining to them with a sigh. "Almost made me want to pick up the phone and call her."

"Well," Brielle spoke up, stacking clothes over her arm. "You should fix that. Or at least reach out. Our moms made us who we are."

Nadia grunted and rolled her eyes as she picked out clothes for Kamaiyah and herself. "Even you," Brielle looked up at her. "You're on this path of healing and you might need to reach back and see if there can be a resolution."

Rolling her eyes, she pursed her lips together and grunted again. "I'm not there, yet, in my healing. The thought of looking her in the face makes my blood boil. But I am all here for Wren talking to her mom and getting that together."

"Well, thank you," Wren was all smiles and it was contagious. The love she wore was beautiful, Roman's growth was beautiful and a love rekindled between the two of them sparked a flame for others to gravitate toward.

"You know, it's about time to plan another group trip. But, if Kwame is bringing Keisha, I don't know if I want to go somewhere, I can't get home on my own," Brielle shared, looking at Nadia who could care less about who Kwame brought along.

"That hoe," Wren winced. The sound of her name made her chest tighten. "I haven't talked to him since that ambush."

"I mean, can you blame him for getting sucked back in? She's pretty." Nadia shrugged her shoulders and walked towards the fitting room where Kamaiyah was trying on the mountains of clothes the girls were gathering for her.

Brielle closed the space between her and Wren and smirked softly. "Something is up with her."

"There's a green monster sitting on her shoulder. But you know she's going to deny it until she's purple in the face. Are we still setting them up?"

Wren chewed on her bottom lip. "We would have to be really slick with it. You know both of them are really skeptical. I have an idea, but we'll talk about it later."

"You're bad," Brielle stepped away, seeing Wren's eyes dance with excitement. "I hope this works out."

"Me, too."

NADIA GARRETT

"IT WOULD'VE BEEN NICE TO KNOW YOU WEREN'T coming into the restaurant today," Nadia rolled her eyes, hearing Kwame's voice through the phone.

"You actually showed up to work today?" Nadia poked her lip out and looked at herself in the mirror at the dress she tried on. Frowning at her reflection, she took the dress off and flung it into the 'no' pile. "I'm off, so make it quick."

"I talked to Isabella, but I wanted you to know, too. Roman plans on proposing to Wren next week. I was hoping you can pull something together at the restaurant for it. If you say no, I got to come out of pocket and hire someone."

She frowned her brow before replying to him. "What makes you think that I was going to do anything for free?"

"Uh... Off of G.P.," Kwame replied with a tinge of confusion in his voice. Judging by Nadia's low laugh, he was wrong. "Damn! G.P. used to get me a long way. The world has changed."

"If we're being honest, G.P. never got you anywhere with me. So, you'll be paying for my services. Because it's Wren, I won't make you come out of pocket too heavy. Is that all you needed?" she asked, ready to hang up on him and return back to having a peaceful afternoon with her girls.

"Uh, yeah... You good?"

"I'm always good, Kwame. Don't be weird," Nadia huffed and placed her hand on her hip. "Is that all?"

"Yeah. Thanks for taking care of the party," he spoke up after a low sigh.

"Anything for my sis," Nadia finalized before hanging up and tossing her phone on the bench covered in clothes. Staring at the phone, she let a small smile creep across her face before she caught herself and groaned. "Bitch, tighten up."

Trying on a few more pieces, she sorted through the things that she wanted and the things she was putting back. After she gathered her items, she walked out of the fitting room with a mountain of clothes in her arms. Bumping into someone, she quickly stepped back and apologized.

"You're good, baby girl," the voice that came from the other side of her pile of clothes caused her to freeze. Her breath went shallow as her heart started to pound against her chest in fright. "Don't act so surprised to see me. You had a conversation with my mother, about time that you and I had one of our own."

Nadia's eyes flooded with tears. In an instant, she returned back to a scared twelve-year-old, wanting someone to save her. "I've been looking everywhere for you. I figured if I made my way around your city enough, I'd find you. I have to thank Isabella for pointing me in the right direction."

"Donte," Nadia searched for her voice but there wasn't any. Just a whimper of a scared child. Only Donte could provoke that reaction from her. She felt like she was twelve all over again.

"Nadia," Kamaiyah spoke from behind her. Hearing her voice snapped her back into herself. "Are you ready?"

Kamaiyah poked her head around the corner for a brief second. Seeing Nadia move towards her, she walked away.

Nadia nodded her head and quickly eased past Donte and scurried to the checkout line. "Are you okay?" Brielle looked at the tears cradled in Nadia's eyes. The last time she saw him, everyone's weekend shifted and she didn't want to do that again. Instead, she forced a smile and placed the clothes on the counter.

"I'm good," she lied to Brielle, who pinned her brows together and looked back at the fitting room and didn't see anyone. "Really, I'm good. Just yawned and you know the tears."

Brielle blinked her suspicions away and looked over at Nadia calming herself. "Where is Wren?"

"Next door with Kamaiyah, getting us a table."

"Have you talked to Julian about next week?" Nadia changed the subject. "Roman is proposing at the restaurant before it opens. So, I might need your help, if you're free."

"Of course. Are you sure you're good?" Brielle asked again.

"Bri," Nadia smiled, turning to look at her. "I'm good. Don't worry about me."

As much as Brielle wanted to believe that, she knew better. She knew Nadia's personality and any time she started to retreat or force herself to smile, there was something bigger happening. For now, she would let it go but her eyes would be on her. "Oh, please! I will always worry about you."

"Don't I know it," Nadia rolled her eyes playfully, after paying for the clothes. "Kamaiyah isn't going to need a thing."

"We are creating a monster. I just need you to know you're going to be the on-call babysitter."

"I love babies, but I give them back before midnight," Nadia smiled. "As long as she knows that, she'll be fine."

22

WREN FRANKLIN

SHE'D GIVEN A LOT OF THOUGHT TO WHAT BRIELLE told her about reconciling with her mother. Since she was healing everything else in her life, her mother was on the list of things that needed to be healed. In order to understand why she was the way she was, she needed to know her story and sympathize with the fact that Terry hadn't always been a good man.

"I can't believe you came to see me," her mother hummed while pouring her a glass of lemonade. "How's everything going with you? You look good."

"So do you," Wren took the glass from her hand and sat down on the couch. Wren looked at her mother's slender figure and her smooth cocoa skin. She had curves that sat in the right places. Her black hair was styled in a pixie haircut that tapered to her round face. She was beautiful, and when they were together, people couldn't tell if they were sisters or mother and daughter. Wren took pride in her mother being a baddie and only hoped that she could look like her at fifty years old.

"I know you've been a little irritated with all the time I've been spending with dad."

Josie sat down in her armchair and laughed before looking at her daughter. "A little irritated... I felt some way about you putting your father on a pedestal."

"What was I supposed to do, Ma?" Wren placed the glass on the coffee table and fell back into the cushions of the couch. "You know how bad I wanted that relationship with my dad."

"So bad that you forgot about your relationship with me." Josie sighed. "It felt like all the hard work and everything I sacrificed disappeared when he showed up on his white horse with his apologies. It was a slap to my face."

"Ma, I didn't know you felt like that," Wren looked at her mother's face. "You were always so hard."

"I had to be. I couldn't show you that I was struggling to keep food on the table and a roof over your head. Thank God for George. He took a lot of that stress off of me," Josie stopped a second to sigh. "You are not wrong for loving your father or even catching up on the missed time. Your father hurt me in ways I never thought I could recover from. He had enough courage to apologize to his kids, which is great. But what about the women he lied to, the women he used to get his way? That's what I'm mad about."

"Mom," Wren spoke up and sighed, shaking her head. "You've been holding on to that for so damn long. I know what we're about to do. Because that is ridiculous. I got to ask, how does George react to that?"

"I never told him. He just thinks I'm mean as hell,"

Josie spoke up, making Wren groan and stare at the ceiling. "He knows that Terry pisses me off but that's about it."

"I swear to God, I get it now. The pain of the mother becomes the affliction of the daughter," Wren chuckled a little, shaking her head and pulled her phone out. She scrolled through her favorites and hit Terry's number. After a few rings, he answered.

"Hey, baby girl! What's going on?"

"Nothing. I'm sitting here with Mom. Did you know she was still mad at you?" Wren asked, looking over at Josie.

"Uh..." Terry started and then sighed. "I could understand why, though. Like I told you, a couple of weeks ago, I regret handling her heart the way I did. She was my rock and I trampled all over her to have my way. Josie..."

"What, Terry?" Josie groaned with her arms folded against her chest.

"Hear me when I tell you I'm sorry," he started. "I was shit. And you never have to forgive me but know that if I could go back and take away all that pain I caused you, I would, in a heartbeat. You have done an amazing job raising Wren. I see so much of you in her. Honestly, that's the reason I latched so tightly onto her. She's my second chance to make it right."

Josie's face softened from her normal hard scowl. "You got to know that your love was too great for me to carry and you sacrificed a lot to make sure she had everything I wasn't there to give her. For that, I will always respect you and I will always love you for that. I'm sorry, Jo. I really mean that, with all my heart. You hear me?"

Josie's eyes fluttered as she chewed on the inside of her cheek. "I hear you, Terry."

"You good?" he asked her.

"I am. Thank you for that." She smiled and looked over at Wren, who nodded her head. "Take care of yourself."

"You too, Josie. Wren, I'll see you later."

"Love you, Daddy. See you later."

Hanging up, she pushed herself up off the couch and went to wrap her arms around her mother. "Stop holding stuff in. You wasted so much life being upset with him."

"Thank you for that. I'm not mad anymore," Josie chuckled, wiping her face.

"Good. Because you and I have a nail appointment. Let's go. Call George and tell him to meet us in the city."

"Wren, I thought you forgot all about me," George spoke from behind his menu.

"G," Wren snickered. "You know I could never forget about you. I've been a little caught up."

"I can see that you're glowing. Who is he and why haven't I met him?" George asked, looking over at his stepdaughter. Their relationship was better now that Wren had come into her own woman and could appreciate another man loving her mother the way she deserved.

"Right now," Wren waved towards the door of the restaurant at Roman. He threw his head her way and walked over to the group seated at the table. "George, this is Roman, my boyfriend."

Roman stopped at George and held his hand out for a firm handshake. Working his way around the table, Josie stood up to hug him. "Boyfriend, huh? He's handsome."

Roman's cheeks flushed red as she released him. "He *must* be something to have you smiling from ear to ear."

"He's everything," Wren grinned as Roman kissed the

top of her head and took his seat beside her. "It hasn't always been like this."

"Always?" Josie's interest was piqued. "Now, I know you haven't been holding out?"

"Mom, you've been mad at me," Wren shrugged.

"Touché," Josie waved her finger and took a sip of her drink.

"So," George started. "Where are you from? What do you do? Why am I just seeing you?"

Wren rolled her eyes. "Here we go."

Roman laughed and took her hand in his. "I'm from Compton, I own a body shop that specializes in custom work and it's pretty profitable. And you're just seeing me now because I was dragging my feet before."

"What made you get your shit together?"

"I lost out the first time around because I wasn't consistent. I had to live without her and that was hell and I promised myself that if she gave me an inch, I was going for the gold," Roman shared, maintaining direct eye contact with George.

"And what's the gold?" Josie asked, looking over at the two hold hands and smile at each other. "Marriage?"

"Of course. That's the goal. I'm not just here to waste her time. Or mine. Life is short and I don't want to waste my time on earth not doing right by her," Roman spoke, proudly looking at Josie, who nodded her head.

George sat up in his seat and studied Roman. He looked at his tattoos and deciphered the meaning behind them. "You said Compton. I'm sure you saw a lot of death."

"I saw it everywhere. A lot of times, it was almost me," Roman shared, unashamed of where he came from or what he had to do to get to this point in his life. Over the last month, he realized that Compton molded him and he couldn't turn his back on the city that made him who he was. He owed them, even if it was just a fraction of what he had. There was some young kid looking for a way out and Roman had the blueprint of how to come out of the haze of the streets.

"Affiliated?" George asked him. Roman nodded his head yes. "Me too. How many homies have you pulled out?"

"None," Roman answered, breaking eye contact for a moment. "If I'm honest... I didn't want to. I felt like I didn't owe them anything. But, the more I'm around my sister and hear stories of how bad it's gotten, I feel like it's time for me to reach back."

"I do some work in Compton, with the youth in the city. We have a job shadowing day planned in a week. How about I help you kick start your give back to the city?" George asked.

"I'm down with it," Roman nodded his head and let a smile creep across his face. "Thank you."

"Anything for a homie."

Josie looked at the two of them shake hands across the table. "I guess it's true what they say, like mother, like daughter. I like him."

"I do, too," Wren laid her head on his shoulder. Looking up at Roman, she smiled. "You won."

"I know I did," Roman returned the gesture and kissed her forehead. "Love you, babe."

"I know you do."

"Roman, you're good in my book. It's always good to see someone from the block who made it out and has a powerful story to tell and has realized that there are other lives that can be saved just by his message alone." George admired the way they were with each other. Their chemistry was organic. Reading Roman, he could tell that he was a man with goals and was on a mission to make his life better. "You're going to do great things."

George could always read people within minutes. He winked at Wren, giving her his seal of approval. She smiled at him and mouthed, "Thank you."

Lifting her head off of Roman's shoulder, she opened her menu. "Now that everyone has given their approval, feed me!"

SHE LOOKED OVER THE ROOM AND SMILED TO HERSELF.
The restaurant was finally finished and she could breathe.
The grand opening was next week and it was full steam
ahead. But, tonight, she was smiling even wider because her
best friend was going to step into another chapter of her life
with the man that finally stuck to his word. Their second
chance at love was beautiful.

"What are you over here thinking about?" Isabella
asked, startling Nadia. "I'm sorry. I didn't mean to scare
you. You've been jumpy all night," she pointed out, looking
at Nadia.

Nadia let her smile fade a little before she sighed. "I'm
just ready for a little bit of rest and have a week of self-care."

"You deserve it. I got you something," Isabella handed
Nadia an envelope. "Please don't talk about how you can't

take it. You've done so much for me, the least I could do is say thank you."

Taking the envelope from her hand, Nadia opened her arms and hugged her. "Thank you."

"You're welcome. After the opening next week, spend a few days of your week of self-care in Catalina," Isabella released her and smiled.

"I'm going to get you! I was thinking it was a gift certificate for nails or something."

"Girl, please." Isabella leaned her body against the bar and looked around at the restaurant that was completely transformed for a private event. Nadia lined the walls of the building with vases of candles to set the mood. Arrangements of peonies, hydrangeas and hyacinths lined the family table in the middle of the floor, which was dressed with white linens, fine china and candles.

"Damn," Kwame whistled, walking into the restaurant. "This is nice."

"I know. Nadia did the damn thing," Isabella cheered along with Kwame. "Remind me to call her when it's my turn."

"Ah, that won't be long. You're dope as hell," Kwame complimented before looking over at Nadia who was still staring at the table. "Nadia."

"Kwame," she greeted politely before walking over the table. Sighing heavily, he looked at Isabella who shooed him towards her.

"Stop being a bitch and go talk to her."

"Ay! Watch your mouth, girl," Kwame warned.

"You're wasting time, Kwame," Isabella groaned and walked away. "He's so damn slow."

Nadia made sure everything on the table was perfect,

all the way down to the name placements. "You don't have to stand there and stare at me."

"I can't enjoy the view?" Kwame smirked, admiring her quietness. "Best table I've seen in a while."

Nadia scoffed and rolled her eyes. "What do you want?"

"A truce."

"No," Nadia mumbled.

"Why not?"

"Because we break those like promises," she spoke up, shaking the fresh curls out her face. "We need to be okay with just being at each other's throats all the time. That's how it's always been, why constantly try to change that?"

"Because," Kwame started. "Fighting with you is exhausting."

"Then, don't," Nadia shrugged. "We have two more restaurants to open and, after that, we go back to being in our own world. No harm, no foul."

Kwame groaned and pinched the bridge of his nose. "You are so damn difficult."

"As opposed to..."

"Will it kill you to be –"

"You didn't have to do it like this," Brielle cheered, walking through the door with Julian behind her. "This is nice."

"Thank you," Nadia walked away like Kwame wasn't even standing there. The only thing she'd managed to do was aggravate him to the tenth power. "Are they on the way?"

"Yeah. Roman said they'll be here in a half hour. Everyone else already pulled up," Julian replied hugging Nadia and then walking over to Kwame.

"This is really nice. I'm so excited," Brielle squealed, clasping her hands together. "Now, the only one left is you."

Nadia waved her off and rolled her eyes. "Don't throw me into that mix."

"I already did."

Roman Daniels

His nerves were running amok as he opened the passenger door for Kamaiyah, then Wren. Holding her hand in his, he nodded for Kamaiyah to go inside. With a smile, she winked at him and walked inside the building.

"You okay?" Wren asked, reaching up to fix his bow tie.

Roman smiled and nodded his head. "Yeah, I'm good. Just ready to eat."

"Well, you know how Isabella does her openings. It's always grand."

"It sure is. Last time, I think you told me to fuck off," Roman chuckled, leading her towards the restaurant after locking the car.

"I did not."

"You put it very nicely. But I'm pretty sure." Rolling her eyes, Wren smacked his shoulder. "But I won. I told you I was going to come back with a vengeance."

"Oh, whatever," Wren hummed as Roman pulled the door open to the restaurant. Everyone stood up and clapped as they walked in. Wren's expression was puzzled as to what was happening but Roman went along with it. She smiled faintly, seeing Terry and Farrah, Josie and George, all their friends and his mother smiling from ear to ear.

"What's going on?" Wren whispered in his ear.

"I won," Roman smirked.

"Won what?" Wren asked, raising her brow. "What is going on?"

The crowd calmed down and watched as Roman brought her knuckles up to his face and kissed them. "I won. I told you to give me a month to prove to you that I wasn't bullshitting with you or your heart. I meant that shit. I'm not wasting my time or yours. I'm not putting anything off in hopes of tomorrow. Tomorrow doesn't belong to us. But today does."

"Roman," Wren warned, as Roman lowered himself to one knee. "Get up."

"Nah! Get that knee dirty, big dawg!" Kwame shouted, causing Julian to bark. Brielle and Nadia rolled their eyes and shook their heads, but their smiles didn't fade as they watched Roman make the biggest move of his life, to date.

"Wren, nothing about my life with you will be fast. Nothing about the way I love you will be rushed. I will go twelve rounds with you, blow for blow, pound for pound. I will love you when it hurts. I will love you when my words fail me. I will love you so damn hard I will lose myself in you. I will love you until the life leaves my body. But I will never leave your side. You've made me a better man and I don't want to be without you." Roman's speech made Wren's eyes swell with tears of joy. Letting her hand go for a brief moment to dig into his pocket, he took the ring out and presented it to her. "Marry me and I will love you better than I did the day before. What do you say?"

"I say yes," she bit down on the corner of her trembling lip. "Yes."

The eruption of cheers and clapping was deafening. They were surrounded by people who loved them without question. People who would coach them through the fight of their lives and never waver.

Standing to his feet, after sliding the ring on her finger, he covered her lips with his. Wren wrapped her hands around his neck and pulled him into a deeper kiss. "I love you."

"I love you."

Love had tested them in ways they never imagined. Fighting for you quickly turned into fighting with you. No matter how hard, how tedious, how extremely difficult it could get, they would fight. Fight until they won and got a love knockout.

***

DINNER HAD CONCLUDED AND, WHILE THE GUESTS were talking, enjoying cake and wine or dancing, Kwame stood at the bar between Julian and Roman.

"I'm proud of you, man," Julian nodded his head. "It's been a hell of a year."

"Sure as hell has." Roman turned around to see Wren dance happily to the music with Nadia and Brielle holding their glasses in their hands. "But we won."

"Leave Kwame out of this," Julian snickered, looking over his shoulder as Isabella approached them.

"I hope you liked everything," she smiled, hugging each of them then taking a step back.

Roman returned the smile and handed her an envelope. "I know you don't take gifts but consider this an investment. Thank you."

"Thank you for trusting me with this. Should I keep my calendar open for the wedding?"

"You should," Roman nodded. "I'm going to steal a

dance with my woman."

Roman excused himself and walked over to the dance floor. Julian decided to join Roman in breaking up the girls' time on the dance floor. Kwame watched as they both pulled them apart. Nadia wasn't left alone too long before Terry began to dance with her. Smirking lightly, he watched a smile cross her face while his father whispered something in her ear.

"You know," Isabella cut in his thoughts, watching him watch Nadia. "You got to stop giving up every time she quips at you and go for the jugular."

"You think so?" he asked, not taking his eyes off of her.

"I think so. You'll figure it out. I have faith in you. Until you do," she nudged his elbow and handed him an envelope. "Take this as my thank you. You and your company stepped in and saved the day for me. I never thought I would have one restaurant, but five... That's a big deal."

"Izzy, *you're* a big deal," Kwame smirked, taking the envelope from her hands. "You're going to do amazing things."

"Thank you. Enjoy a few days in Catalina on me. Kick back, unwind and reset. I'll see you when you get back."

Kwame pulled her into a hug and kissed the top of her head. "Thanks. Try not to get into trouble while I'm gone."

"I plan on taking a bit of a vacation myself."

"Good! You deserve it."

"Oh, and Kwame," Isabella spoke up again. "You should try to be alone for this trip. Do some self-reflecting."

Kwame smirk and nodded his head. He would self-reflect but he had no intentions on doing it alone.

The End for Now...

EPILOGUE

The Winner's Circle

Fight for me
Keep it on lock for me
Keep it sacred for me

Fight for us
Keep it going for us
Keep it pure for us

Our fight was never supposed to be easy
Our fight was never supposed to be clean
Cookie cutter, sugar covered and pristine

Our fight got ugly
I wanted to give up
Tired of swinging
Tired of going back and forth
Tired of the gut punches, side jabs and right hooks
Tired of you not knowing my worth

Nothing about this was smooth
Nothing about this was pain-free
Gut-wrenching pain down on my bended knee
Everything about this was worth it

Standing here with you
Standing with me
Standing for us

The winners circle
Congratulations
You won...you got it
You fought a good fight
Took me out after twelve rounds

Keep your gloves on
Because now we fight together against the world
And any devices wanting to take us down

I'm yours and you'll forever be mine

A.P.

AFTERWORD

Thank you for reading. The final installment is up next. Kwame and Nadia have a difficult start, but once love enters the equation, will it be smooth sailing or a fight for their lives? Find out in book 3 of Love, The Series, *Fight for Love*.

Until next time. Live, love, grow.

- A.P.

ALSO BY AUBREÉ PYNN

Thank you for reading! Make sure you check out my catalog:

Dope Boys I&II

Everything is Love

Mistletoe Meltdown

My Love for You

My Love for You, Always

Say He'll Be My Valentine

The Way You Lie

The Way You Lie: The Aftershock

Run from Me

Love Over All

The Game of Love

Connect with me on my social media:

IG: @aubreepynn

TWITTER: @aubreepynn

Facebook: Aubreé Pynn

Check out my website:

Aubreepynnwrites.wordpress.com

A million words, in a million books is never thank you enough for your support.

CPSIA information can be obtained
at www.ICGtesting.com
Printed in the USA
LVHW111450011119
636084LV00003B/420/P